MORE THAN HUMAN

by
Heather Ashbury

I

More Than Human

Copies of the book may be ordered through booksellers or by contacting

Author Heather Ashbury
PO BOX 6
GILA, NM 88038

Rev. date 11/27/20

Acknowledgements

For Dana who has been like a mother to me

To my loving husband, to my dad, and to all those who encouraged me and supported me through this project, thank you.

Front Cover designed by: Kelsey Jordan IG: @shade.16k

Table of Contents:

"It's simply marvelous, to me, how the damaged ones seem to find each other through subtleties unbeknownst to them."
-Unknown

CHAPTER 1

The funeral service came to an end. The air was thick, heavy with mourning and grief. One by one the pews emptied as loved ones, friends, and family formed a line in front of the casket where Jeff's body lied. Jule straightened her modest black dress and made her way, politely finding her place in the line. Giving a quick scan of the room for the first time since her arrival, she recognized a few old friends from her time spent in New Mexico a few years ago. As she looked ahead, she noticed Jeff's mother, father, and sister standing at the side of the dark chestnut casket, holding each other in a most sorrowful embrace. Jule hadn't been formally acquainted with his family, although they had been good friends for many years. She yearned to say something to them, to give them some words of comfort and express to them how much she enjoyed their son, but she hesitated and decided to pass them by without a word, giving a polite smile as she slowly approached the ornate casket to pay her respects.

The service in all was beautiful and touching. Jeff's casket was gorgeous, liberally adorned with red and white carnations accompanied with fern accents splayed out across the top. His somber face was brightly illuminated by the late morning sun shining through the colorful stained-glass window of the church – the only element giving any notion of life to him. She frowned as she looked down at his resting body. *This isn't Jeff. This is just a* shell *of Jeff,* she came to realize. Her eyes began to well up and a tear gently rolled down her cheek as she remembered his bright blue eyes that were so full of life and his contagious smile that could lift the dampened spirits of any room. She would never truly understand why he took his own life; why he left so much behind. It didn't feel right to her. All she knew was that there would be an empty void where Jeff's happiness and infectious joy had once inhabited.

She took a deep breath, wiped away a tear and forced a smile.

"Until next time, my friend," she said quietly. "I will miss you."

She gently placed her hand on top of his for a moment, feeling his cold lifelessness, before making her way through the crowd of mourners for the exit. As Jule walked toward the doors of the church, a familiar blond-haired man with light blue eyes and a pierced eyebrow smiled as he quickly approached her, opening the door.

"Loki!" she exclaimed. "It's great to see you. Well, maybe not under these circumstances, but nonetheless, it makes me happy to see your face again." Jule mustered a quick grin.

Loki smiled back as they made their way outside.

A massive summer thunderstorm raged on as if the gods themselves were angry with the world. Thunder crashed, echoing and rumbling all around as lightning struck a nearby hilltop. The pouring rain began quickly flooding the parking lot. The tumultuous wind forcibly thrashed the trees back and forth, testing their mobility and strength. Jule braced herself for the wind and cold rain, crossing her arms tightly over her chest.

"My car is parked right over there." She projected her voice over the commotion of the storm and pointed to her blue car. "Let's go talk out of the rain."

Loki nodded in agreement. Jule, prepared for the unpredictable weather of New Mexico, extended her umbrella, doing her best to shield them both as they hurriedly made their way to her car. They quickly climbed inside and closed the doors, Jule taking a little more time to put away her umbrella.

"So," she said as they settled in their seats, "what have you been up to? It's been a long time."

"It's been, what, three years since you went back to Phoenix?" he asked as he slid a cigarette out of his pack, and then gestured it to Jule, offering her one. She hesitantly accepted and cracked the windows, some rain finding its way into the car and splashing onto her face.

"Yeah, just about I guess," she replied after lighting her cigarette and taking a long drag, slowly blowing the smoke out of her mouth and nostrils.

"Do you ever regret it? Leaving, I mean?"

"Actually, I do," she said longingly. "I thought that moving back to Phoenix would open up some new opportunities for me, but, as it turns out, I'm just more lonely and unhappy there. I don't think I belong in the big city… I feel like I'm choking on all that smog, surrounded by all those people. Even though that's where I was raised and that's where my oldest friends are, I feel disconnected, in a sense." She paused for a moment and looked out her window. The rain lightened into a slight drizzle, the thunder quieted, and the wind had become a gentle breeze. A small break in the clouds began to form and the sun peered down once again.

"This place," she continued, "I've never felt anything like I do when I'm here. I feel free. I feel like I can breathe. I feel like I'm home." Jule shrugged.

"Well that's good." Loki smiled. "Have you thought about moving back?"

Jule chuckled lightly as she exhaled smoke. "Well, I've thought about it. I just don't know when or how I could. I'd have no place to stay, I have a roommate in Phoenix, I'm in-between jobs right now, and I might as well be broke. I barely even had enough money to make the trip out here for the funeral. I'm probably going to have to borrow some money just to make it back, honestly."

"That's okay, we could make it work," Loki said optimistically. "My brother and I own a bar now. You could come and work for us, and I'm sure Lillith would love to have you stay with her for a while. That is, if you'd like to stay here rather than return to that cesspool of a city."

A glint of excitement struck Jule as she considered Loki's offer. If she was being honest with herself, she really was looking for *any* reason to leave Phoenix and return to New Mexico. Maybe this was it.

"You know, that's a great idea. You'd really do that for me?" Jule's eyes lit up.

"Of course I would. You belong here, with us." Loki smiled reassuringly. "By the way, I'm having a gathering at my house tonight. Kind of an honor to Jeff's memory. A bunch of us will be there. I think you should come. It'll be fun," he persuaded her with a mischievous grin.

"Yeah, okay, that sounds good. It would be nice to reconnect with everyone again. Who is going to be there?"

"Oh, a bunch of people that knew Jeff. A lot of people you used to party with, actually," Loki replied. "I think Rayme even convinced William to go." Loki smirked and glanced at Jule waiting to see what reaction saying his name would bring.

Her cheeks immediately flushed bright red.

"Yeah I'll definitely be there. It's at your place, right? Same spot?"

"Yes," Loki confirmed. "I'll see you this evening."

"Sounds good."

Loki leaned over the center console and gave Jule a hug before exiting her car.

"I really hope you come," he added. "It's really important."

Loki slammed the door shut as he walked away. Jule started the engine and pulled out of the parking lot, turning onto the highway that led to Lillith's house a few miles outside of town. With her window still cracked, she breathed in the refreshing, coniferous mountain air, letting out a relaxed sigh. She freed her long brown hair from her ponytail, the wind tossing it about in a wild frenzy, and turned the volume dial all the way up, blasting her heavy metal music. The road curved and bent flowing with the landscape, rocking the car gently back and forth as she navigated the mountainside.

CHAPTER 2

Reaching the end of the pavement, Jule slowed her vehicle, cruising slowly down the dirt road until she came upon a house marked with a bright purple mailbox. She arrived at Lillith's and pulled the car into the open driveway.

Two happy dogs, one brown and white mutt, the other a German shepherd, ran up and greeted Jule with whines of excitement and licks of love. Jule grinned as she greeted the dogs in return with pats on the head and scratches down their backs. The front screen door of the main house swung open and Lillith, wearing a loose-fitting floral sundress and walking around barefoot as usual, stepped out onto the porch. She was cradling a baby swaddled in her arms.

"Jule!" Lillith exclaimed with a wave. "What a pleasant surprise! I didn't know you were in town. Why didn't you call me?" she asked, placing her hand on her hip in a sassy manner.

Jule smiled cheerfully as she walked up the short stairs to Lillith's porch and embraced her tightly with a hug. "Hey, I'm sorry I didn't call. I just figured you would be home. Even if you weren't, this is a nice drive," Jule said as she looked around. She peered down at the baby bundled in a blanket peacefully asleep in Lillith's arms. She beamed as she gently brushed her finger along the infant's cheek.

"Who is this cute little thing?"

"This is my newest daughter, Abigail." Lillith said proudly. "She just turned four-months-old last week."

"Four months already! She is super cute – she looks just like you!"

"She better!" Lillith sassed back. "My other one, you know, Xena, looks just like her daddy. It drives me nuts!" They both laughed.

"Where is she?" Jule asked, glancing around.

"She's over at a friend's house and won't be back until this evening. I needed a break, you know?" Lillith chuckled. "Why don't you come inside? Let's catch up and I'll make some coffee. I really need to put Abigail down – she's killing my arms."

Jule followed Lillith into the house, carefully maneuvering her way through the living room, stepping around the chaos of toys splayed out carelessly on the floor to an old green couch, sinking into it as she sat down. Lillith disappeared around the corner with her baby. Three years had passed since she last saw Lillith, but she hadn't changed one bit, Jule noted. Lillith was a few inches taller than her petite self. She had dark brown hair that flowed in a wave down to her hips and she wore a broken pair of glasses that were held together in the middle with tape. She was so welcoming and treated Jule like a sister, which meant a lot to her as she was estranged from her blood family. For her, her friends *were* family – part of the reason why she wished to return to New Mexico so much. Ever since she was a child she struggled to fit in, never really finding her niche until she moved to New Mexico shortly after high school. Here, it didn't take long for her to find and make friends, discovering a whole group of individuals who appreciated her for her, with all her quirks and differences. Everything that made Jule feel like she was weird were things that her friends found endearing and loved about her.

Jule only had one real, close friend in Phoenix like that: her roommate Annabelle. Jule and Annabelle grew up in the same neighborhood together and met as young children at a local park, becoming fast, inseparable friends. They shared their most intimate secrets with one another and spent all of their free time together. She loved and already missed her beautiful friend. Jule admitted she had always been a little jealous of Annabelle's grace, her elegant gait, her glimmering green eyes, her perfect figure, and gorgeous, thick, long dirty blonde hair. She had a bold presence that naturally demanded attention and a powerful confidence. Though Jule was envious at times, she never let it get between their friendship. Although Annabelle was incredibly gorgeous, she was also very humble about her appearance. She never flaunted her beauty or made Jule feel inferior to her in any way. Jule adored absolutely everything about her friend. She was the only thing making her hesitate when considering a move back to New Mexico. She didn't want to leave her best friend behind and she felt like she was abandoning her. This idea was weighing heavily on her, though the pros seemed to vastly outweigh the cons. It was a decision that would not come lightly or easily.

Maybe I could convince Annabelle to move out here someday, Jule thought to herself. *I just know that she would love it here.*

Lillith returned with two cups of coffee in her hands and sat down next to Jule. They exchanged small talk as they sipped on their drinks in Lillith's quaint living room. It was decorated in every possible crevice with houseplants, ornate pentagrams, bells, and other occult decorations. Lillith openly practiced witchcraft. Her lifestyle intrigued Jule, though she never had the bravery to delve into such mysterious things. Lillith's talents were in the realm of divination, using tools like runes and tarot cards to reveal situations to her and provide guidance. Jule never believed any of that stuff, but enjoyed watching Lillith practice anyway.

"I was going to ask you," Jule said after a pause in their conversation, "if it's not too much of a bother, could I stay in your guest house for a little while? I have an opportunity to move back here. Loki's going to set me up with a job and I just need a place to stay until I can get on my feet."

"Jule, of course you're welcome to stay here!" Lillith exclaimed as she placed a hand on Jule's knee. "I'm so happy you're considering moving back! You know, you really belong here. You can stay here as long as you need to and I'll be more than happy to feed you. Ooh and I can do a reading for you!" Lillith smirked and nudged Jule with her elbow.

Jule leaned forward and gave Lillith an appreciative, tight hug and thanked her. Lillith was someone she could always count on to be there for her.

"So what brought you back this time?"

Jule set her coffee down on the table and leaned back, curling her legs up on the couch.

"A friend passed away. I came back to attend the funeral." Jule frowned. "By the way, can I use your bathroom to change my clothes?"

Lillith respectfully dropped the topic.

"I'm so sorry, Jule," she said. She leaned forward to give Jule another hug. "Of course, the bathroom is just down the hall, second door on the left."

Jule thanked Lillith once again went out the front door to her car to grab her things. As she made her way into the bathroom, her phone rang.

CALL FROM ANNABELLE, her phone displayed.

She answered, juggling it between her shoulder and ear as she set her bag down.

"Hello?"

"Hey, Jule. How's everything going?"

"Oh, not too bad, I guess. The funeral was nice, but sad, and I saw a few friends. I'm actually going to a memorial party with a bunch of them later, so that's cool," Jule replied with forced enthusiasm in an attempt to hide her hurting heart.

"That's nice," Annabelle said. "So, what are you doing now? When are you coming back?"

"Well, at the moment I'm visiting at a friend's house. I think I'm going to be staying here for a while, maybe about two weeks. Then I'm thinking I might move back here permanently," Jule hesitated, breaking the news to her friend. "But on the bright side, you don't have to kick me out and it gives you a chance to find a better roommate. You know, one who actually has a job, makes money, and can help cover the bills." She tried to be optimistic about the situation.

Annabelle sounded disappointed regardless. "Really? You're moving away again?"

"Yeah, I think I am. I'm sorry! My friend Loki owns a bar here with his brother and he's going to set me up with a job. Another friend has a place for me to stay for a while until I can get on my feet. It's worked out so well, it almost seems like I'm supposed to move back here, you know? Everyone keeps saying I belong here. Maybe I do. You know I never really liked it in Phoenix. I'm actually a lot happier here. I'm not even sure why I left in the first place…" Jule trailed off in thought.

"Well that sucks," Annabelle mumbled. "Maybe I can visit you! Where in New Mexico are you again?"

"I'm around Tall Pines. It's a small town in the mountains," Jule replied as she began getting undressed. "Hey, I'm going to have to let you go. I need to finish changing and then head to that memorial party. Call me later though, okay? I'll see you again in about two weeks when I come back to get my stuff."

"Sure, sounds great. I hope you have fun. I miss you already!"

Jule hung up the phone, placed it back in her bag, and finished changing, carefully folding her funeral dress and placing it gently in her backpack, zipping it shut.

How sweet of Annabelle to check up on me, she thought to herself.

Relaxed and finally comfortable in her typical attire of a t-shirt, jeans, and military style boots, Jule exited the bathroom and plopped back down on the couch next to Lillith. The girls continued their conversation, going over all their life's little details until Jule looked at the clock and realized that it was time for her to go. She removed her bags from her car and set them on the bed in the guest house located a few yards to the right of the main house. Jule hugged Lillith goodbye, got in her car, and made her way down the windy road back to town.

MORE THAN HUMAN

CHAPTER 3

Jule pulled her car up to the curb in front of Loki and Bradley's two-story colonial style home. It was an antique white house with a wraparound porch. Conveniently located in a quaint and quiet neighborhood, it was surrounded by a typical, cute picket fence with a lush green grassy lawn that one would see in homeowner's magazines. A few shady trees and fruit trees dotted the yard, the fruit trees just beginning to bear fruit in the mid-summer. Jule stepped out of her car and passed through a small gate under an archway of vines, making her way up the red brick pathway that parted the grass. She went up the small set of stairs to the antique, brown front door. Jule tapped gently on the glass, awaiting a reply.

Bradley, the shorter and stockier brother of Loki, opened the door. Loki and Bradley shared the same eyes and color of hair, but Loki was tall and slender, whereas Bradley was a modest size with a muscular build. Though his appearance was intimidating to anyone who didn't know him, Bradley was really quite the gentle soul.

"Jule!" he exclaimed with a big jolly smile. He grabbed her up off the ground in a strong, tight hug and swung her back and forth. "Oh I've missed you so much, Little One!" he said as he put her back down on her feet. "Little One" was an endearing nickname the group bestowed on Jule, playing off her petite size, but Bradley used it more than anyone else.

Jule stumbled forward slightly, laughing as her feet hit the ground. "I've sure missed your big ol' bear hugs."

"Come in! Come in!" He waved her inside and closed the door behind her.

Jule passed through the threshold, the old hard wooden floors creaking beneath her feet with every step. The delicious smell of cooking food floated through the air and filled her nostrils making her salivate.

"Oh my," she said. "That smells divine! What are you guys cooking? I'm starving!"

"Loki is fixing up some burgers and dogs. We've got plenty of food if you're hungry," Bradley replied, leading Jule through the entryway and living room into the kitchen. "Snacks are over there and drinks are in the cooler. Help yourself."

Loki was busily working back and forth, obviously overwhelmed and frustrated. He glanced up and greeted Jule, giving her a wave with the spatula in his hand, and hurriedly continued his work. Jule, having not eaten anything since early that morning before her trip to Tall Pines, eagerly helped herself to a heaping pile of chips on a paper plate and a soda. Afterward, she followed Bradley outside to the front porch.

"We should really stay out of his way," Bradley whispered. They went down the porch stairs onto the lush green carpet of grass. "You know how he gets."

"Still 'King of the Kitchen'?" Jule asked facetiously. Bradley nodded and they both chuckled.

Jule indulged in her snacks as they sat on the plastic lawn chairs in the cool grass and waited for the other guests to arrive. The sun was just beginning to set. Color burst through the sky with brilliant red and orange hues as lightning danced beneath looming thunderheads billowing in the distance. The sinking sun silhouetted the dark thunderheads with magnificent golden rays above the pink-tipped mountains on the western horizon. A light wind picked up and the temperature suddenly dropped, sending a chill through Jule's body. Within moments, the glorious show of color ended, fading into gloomy gray.

"So, how many people are you guys expecting? That's quite a bit of food Loki is cooking," Jule remarked.

"Oh, it's not that there are a lot of people coming. It's that those who are coming have famously enormous appetites," Bradley laughed. "Loki can eat like a horse himself. Then Athan, Demonik, Azul, Viktor, Rayme, and William are supposed to be coming," he counted on his fingers. "I'm actually not sure if we have enough food."

Jule's heart fluttered at the mention of William again. She's privately had feelings for him that she couldn't explain ever since they were first introduced several years ago. Meeting in a class during her first year at the University of Tall Pines, they became fast friends spending long hours in each other's company. Jule's low self-esteem and lack of confidence prevented her from making any attempt to tell William how she felt, or that she felt anything at all, for that matter. To her, he was out of her league. Sure they were great friends, best friends even, but Jule believed that was all they would ever be. Her heart sank at the thought. Though she believed she could never be with William in the way she imagined, she appreciated the friendship they had and was thrilled at the thought of seeing him again.

Jule swallowed down the rest of her soda and let out an involuntary burp. Bradley glanced over at her and laughed. Jule shrugged it off like no big deal.

"So, Bradley, how's life?"

"Lonely." he stated solemnly. "I spend a lot of time with my brother, but he can't give me the companionship I'm looking for, if you catch my drift. This town is just too small and my choices of women here are very slim. I'm afraid I'll never find anyone. I'm going to be alone forever."

Jule frowned.

"That's not true!" she said. "People come in and out of this town all the time. It's a college town, so chicks come from all over the place to go to school here. Owning that bar and working there, you're bound to meet someone! You're such a sweet, intelligent guy. You deserve someone great, someone worthy of you," Jule encouraged.

"That's very sweet of you to say."

Lighting a cigarette and leaning back in the lawn chair she watched as headlights approached from the top of the hill. A maroon sedan slowly pulled up to the curb, the brakes giving a squeak as it came to a stop behind Jule's car. A tall, slender woman with short auburn hair, fair skin, and very risqué clothing stepped out of the driver's side. A tall man extravagantly decorated with tattoos and piercings, dark sunglasses concealing his eyes, wearing all black baggy clothing with long black hair to match stepped out of the front passenger side of the car. A slightly shorter, thin man wearing a gray pinstriped fedora with a long black vulture feather stuffed in the mauve band, equally decorated with piercings and tattoos as the first man, matching with his black attire and a long trench coat that dragged on the ground behind him, stepped out of the back passenger side of the car. Catarina, Demonik, and Viktor approached Bradley and Jule on the lawn.

"There are two of the hungry men now!" Bradley exclaimed as he got up in greeting. "And of course, the ever-so-eloquent Catarina," he added with a bow.

"Hey guys," Jule said as she stood up and gave a friendly wave, trying to be polite.

Jule wasn't very eager to see these three. Out of this group of friends Jule grew to be a part of, Demonik, Catarina, and Viktor gave her the most uneasy feeling. Demonik's brother, Azul, made her even more nervous and she was glad he didn't tag along. There was something about Catarina in particular that made Jule feel as if she couldn't trust her, but she couldn't quite put her finger on what it was. Following her gut instinct, she made a conscious effort into keeping some distance between them and made sure to never divulge any sensitive information to her or to get too intimate.

Viktor was a dark person, that's the best way Jule could explain it to herself. He was mysterious, unpredictable, and extremely violent if he ever lost his temper, which happened often. Demonik, however, was the least threatening of the three. He seemed more lost than anything. As if he was aimlessly wandering the world, not sure of who he was or of his purpose on earth. Jule found it odd how quickly Catarina sprung on Demonik after the tragic passing of his girlfriend several years ago. He had never been the same since. Jule seemed to be the only one in the group concerned with Catarina's true intentions towards Demonik after such a travesty happened to him. It was suspicious to her. However, she felt it best to keep her suspicions to herself so as not to be seen as "jealous" or paranoid by the others. She felt that no one would really listen to her anyway, so her words would be a waste.

"Your brother isn't coming?" Jule asked Demonik, wanting to confirm that Azul would indeed be absent that night.

"No, Azul had to work. He's a bouncer at a nightclub now, so he works most nights," Demonik replied in his deep and naturally menacing voice. Catarina clung to his arm possessively, never letting Demonik wander very far from her. She gave Jule a subtle, quick, threatening glare with her soulless brown eyes. Catarina was an overly territorial woman. She was cold, narcissistic and aggressive. Demonik was hers and she made sure that everyone knew. Catarina had a habit of hissing at other women who dared to even glance at Demonik and occasionally went as far as scratching like a wild cat if the hissing didn't ward them off fast enough.

"Let's go inside and get some food, everyone else should be arriving soon," Bradley said as he ushered them all back inside the house. Jule took one last drag before stamping out her cigarette into the grass and meandered slowly behind.

As the group went inside, classic rock music was playing quietly in the background and Loki was standing proudly next to his delicious edible display presented on the large dining room table. The new arrivals picked up plates and helped themselves to the food as Jule took a seat on the couch alone in the living room. A knock pounded on the door.

"I'll get it," Loki announced. He placed his plate of food down and opened the door. Athan, a very tall man with thinning blond hair that lightly extended past his shoulders, stepped in. He towered next to Loki and was easily the tallest member of the group. He had a peculiar awkwardness about him in the way that he carried himself which really made him stand out. Loki and Athan exchanged hugs and moved aside. Dwarfed by Athan's great height, two smaller girls entered the house behind him, one slightly taller than the other. Jule recognized them both immediately and excitedly ran over to greet and hug them.

"Esadora! Fidelia!" Jule exclaimed as she eagerly embraced her friends. Esadora, the smaller of the two, had short dark brown hair, enchanting deep brown doe eyes, and beautiful supple red lips. Her light brown, flawless skin, and a perfect hourglass figure made her irresistible to men and women alike. Even Jule was drawn to her. Esadora could easily be a model if she so chose, but she was far too shy for such a self-idolizing position. Jule secretly envied her natural goddess-like beauty. In her eyes, she didn't compare to the natural beauty of her friend.

Fidelia was a thin, spunky girl with fiery red hair to match her personality. Her hair was always a mess and "had a mind of its own", as Fidelia herself once described it. She had hypnotic green eyes that, to Jule, reminded her of a cat's eyes. They were haunting and deep, but mystical and playful at the same time. She had pale, freckle-kissed skin and long, slender limbs.

Jule shared quite a lot in common with both Esadora and Fidelia. The three formed a special bond with each other over the years.

The guests mingled together throughout the house chatting and eating as they waited for the last, straggling guests to arrive. Loki brought out a special framed photo of Jeff and placed it in the center of the mantelpiece with an arrangement of unlit candles and flowers as he prepared for the memorial.

Another knock on the door alerted the crowd that the last expected guests had finally arrived. Bradley stood up from his seat near the coffee table and opened the door to two skinny men standing side by side.

"Hey Rayme come on in! William, you made it!" Bradley again hugged and greeted the guests as he politely invited them inside.

Rayme was a tall young man with short brown hair and dark brown eyes. He wore a pair of square-framed glasses that magnified his eyes and he never went anywhere without his beloved book bag slung heavily over his shoulder. Being a genius botanist, he was constantly studying and learning the medicinal properties for various plants and how to cultivate them as well as experimenting with cross-breeding plants for more concentrated effects. Jule admired his immense desire for knowledge.

Jule, too caught up in her conversation with Esadora to notice, broke off mid-sentence as Esadora gently nudged her arm and nodded her head in William's direction as he entered the room. She looked up and met his gaze, her heart pounding in her chest. His eyes seemed to peer straight into her soul. Her heart skipped a beat as she smiled sheepishly and he approached them.

Does literally everyone know that I have a thing for William? Jule asked herself in embarrassment. *Does he know?*

They greeted each other and he embraced her with a tight, intimate hug. William towered over her standing at 6'1, but then again Jule was a petite woman herself, so who didn't tower over her? He had long, lean muscular arms and legs with a farmer's tan that Jule thought was *adorable*. She admired his strong jawline and pleasant masculine features. She could feel his heart beat against her cheek as she rested her head on his chest, squeezing him tightly in return. His heart quickened its pace, thumping in unison with her own. His cologne filled her nostrils; it was intoxicating. She felt weak in the knees and a flutter in her stomach. She made sure not to make her attraction too obvious and acted as casual as possible, but deep down she wished she could stay in his arms for eternity, ignoring the rest of the world. She was undeniably and completely infatuated with him, if not completely in love with him, but Jule wasn't brave enough to admit that to herself. He looked down at her with his piercing blue eyes, the green circles surrounding the pupil nearly glowed. He gave a subtle wink, causing Jule to involuntarily blush.

Keep your cool, she reminded herself. They stepped apart and took their seats near each other on the enormous couch in front of the mantle next to Esadora and Fidelia.

"Alright everyone, listen up please!" Loki announced over the chatter as he clanged a silver fork against a dark green ceramic coffee mug held in his left hand.

The group gathered in the living room, quieted down, found their places to sit, and gave Loki their attention.

"Now, I invited you all here because every one of us has one main thing in common: Jeff was a great friend to all of us," he continued saying as he approached the mantle. He removed a lighter from his pocket and began lighting the candles surrounding the photo of Jeff – a picture taken at a party Jule attended a few years ago of him standing in a doorway looking back and smiling his infectious smile.

"Jeff was such a loving, kind, and giving person," Loki continued. "He's the type of guy who would literally give you the shirt off his back. He's the guy you could call at two in the morning if you were lonely or sad and he would never hesitate to help make you feel better. Jeff was a one-of-a-kind guy, and this world lost a true treasure." Loki paused for a moment, tears welling up in his eyes as he spoke of his dearly departed friend. The room was silent and still. Tears also welled up in Jule's eyes as she remembered all of the kind things Jeff did for her and how genuine of a person he really was.

Loki cleared his throat before continuing his speech.

"I would like to take a moment now and go around the room and have us all, one-by-one, share an important memory of Jeff. Let us remember him fondly."

Everyone respectfully took a turn to share a profound memory of Jeff. Some were funny, some were sad, others were touching. When Esadora, the last of the group to share, finished describing her favorite memory, Loki and Bradley both approached the mantle in unison and blew out the candles, then stood on either side to face the crowd.

"There's another reason I have invited you all here tonight," Loki began with a more serious tone. "I have discussed this topic with a few of you, but now I think it's time to bring it out into the open to the rest of you."

Jule was lost. *What could Loki be talking about,* she wondered to herself. She shot a glance at Esadora for a hint who simply gave a shrug of her shoulders.

Loki looked at his brother and Bradley returned a nod of approval before he continued.

"This first bit may shock some of you, but please keep any comments to yourself until I am finished." He paused again, the anticipation building in his attentive audience. Jule started shaking her leg, annoyed and impatient. "Jeff did not commit suicide. He was murdered." Loki's astounding announcement sent a buzzing of whispers throughout the room, everyone mumbling and quietly arguing among each other, all except for Jule who grew still and stared at the photo of Jeff in front of her in silence, her ears ringing, the commotion around her fading into a soft hum.

Loki's words took Jule by surprise, but it supported her suspicion of Jeff's mysterious death. According to what she had heard, he went to another state to visit some family, had too much to drink one night and ended up in a fatal, intentional wreck. Jeff was known to drink, but he was always such a responsible person. Driving intoxicated violated one of his most important rules. The thought of him knowingly risking his life and the lives of others from driving drunk was not typical behavior for Jeff. Some said that something happened to make him upset which sent him off in his drunken escapade, but that just didn't seem right to Jule, either. Jeff was a very calm and rational individual and was often used as a mediator for any problems the group had with each other.

"Please," Loki begged as he motioned to the crowd with his hands to settle down. "Let me finish."

The buzzing of voices immediately died down.

"Jeff did not commit suicide," he continued. "Jeff was murdered. I know the stories that have circulated suggest that he drove into a tree on purpose while intoxicated, but I can assure you that was not the case. I cannot provide you with sufficient tangible evidence to back this claim, you just have to trust me. I know he was murdered and we are all in danger."

Loki turned his eyes to Jule and stepped towards her. Jule sat confused and nervous. Why was Loki singling her out? Everyone watched as he knelt down in front of her to meet her at eye-level. She shifted uncomfortably in her seat.

"Now, Jule, there is something that you need to know, something that you should have been told a long time ago but we never really felt the time was right. Now we have no choice and you need to be warned. The information I am about to tell you is going to seem wild and completely impossible, but I tell you, it is possible. You must believe me."

The sincerity in Loki's voice shook Jule and she was taken aback. She didn't know how to make sense of that. Sense of what exactly – she didn't even know. *What's going on?* Jule looked at William, her trusted friend, with uncertainty in her eyes, her hands uncontrollably trembling. Her anxiety rising and getting the better of her. William softened his gaze. He scooted closer to her and gently placed his arm around her, doing what he thought would make her feel safe. She absorbed the room; all eyes were fixed on her. She looked back at Loki and waited for him to continue.

"When you first arrived here years ago, I, and others, felt your presence. I knew another like us had arrived," Loki said as he gestured with his hands to everyone around the room. "So I sent out Athan to find you. You two became friends very quickly, as expected, and then we met, and you met the rest of the group. We all discussed you – debated whether you were just a human or not." Loki paused, giving time to allow Jule's mind to absorb what he had just said to her.

Human or not? What does he mean by that? Jule found herself at a loss for words but flooded with a million questions. She remained silent and patiently waited for Loki to continue.

"For the most part, we agree that you are not human."

Jule noticed Viktor roll his eyes hard to the side and snicker.

"Jule, *I* believe there is more to you than you know. I would like to show you – *we* would like to show you – to educate you, guide you, and prepare you in your journey of discovering your True Self. We feel that it is time for you to know the truth, to know who you really are and who we really are."

"Are we going to show her now?" Viktor asked with a seething grin and a sinister glimmer in his eye, rubbing his hands together eagerly.

Jule's eyes widened. *This is impossible*, she thought. This was getting to be too much and too weird. She felt uncomfortable. Uneasy.

"No." Loki's reply was quick and stern. "I think we've put enough shock and confusion into her for one day."

Viktor frowned and dropped his hands to his lap, obviously disappointed in being told no.

"Don't be afraid." Loki turned back to Jule. "We are still your friends, we just have secrets, as everyone does. Our secrets just happen to have a little more, flare." Loki smiled.

Jule admitted she was feeling a little afraid and very unsure. It was a strange situation. They were all so sincere, so serious. Not a single smirk or laugh in the room. She felt like a stranger among them, no longer recognizing the people that she called her friends.

"I understand this is a lot to take in," Loki said, placing his hand gently on Jule's shoulder. Fidelia and Esadora scooted closer to Jule and hugged her as William took Jule's hand. She was so overwhelmed by this new information that she didn't even realize that William was holding her hand. She felt numb and disconnected.

"You guys are serious?" she finally asked as she looked around. Everyone nodded in unison, collectively admitting that they were all indeed serious. Jule took a deep breath. "So, what are you then? Aliens? What am I?"

"No, we're not aliens," Loki chuckled. "That's a little more complicated to explain. We are all different and have our own uniqueness, as do you. Please, I want you to come back tomorrow and I can explain much more, but right now I need to warn you." Loki's tone became more paternal. "Jeff was murdered by a member of a group called The Order of Purity. A barbaric religious group whose sole purpose is to hunt down other beings like us. When Jeff was away visiting family, a member of the Order somehow tracked him down, killed him, and made it look like he intentionally drove head-on into a tree. We're not exactly sure how they did it, but they could be after us next. Which also means you."

Loki stood up to address everyone in the room.

"If Jeff was discovered, it wouldn't be very difficult for the Order to trace him back to here, looking for more of us and finding *us*. We all need to be careful and cautious. Watch your back, watch what you're saying, watch who you're talking to, and most of all watch what you're doing." He shot a quick look of warning to Viktor. "We all knew that this day would eventually come." Loki seemed to be directing his last statement to both Demonik and Viktor who grinned at each other. Jule noticed their mischievous expressions. *Those two are trouble*, she thought to herself.

"You two need to relay this information back to Azul until I have a chance to explain the situation to him myself." Loki pointed his long index finger at the sinister duo.

The room began to buzz again as the worried crowd expressed their concerns and hashed out plans. Jule remained silent, still in awe and disbelief. She didn't feel afraid anymore, surprisingly, but found herself more in disbelief. The warning of possible danger from Loki hadn't even registered yet.

"Not human." These words repeated over and over in Jule's head as she tried to make any sense of it. She felt like she was in some strange sort of altered dream-state with the room beginning to spin about her.

"I need some air," she announced to no one in particular as she got up to leave the ruckus and headed out the door. She sought the quiet solitude of the night to still her chaotic mind. She leaned heavily against the railing letting out a big sigh. A gentle zephyr picked up and carried the chilly night air through Jule's hair sending a shiver down her spine. She greedily inhaled a deep breath of the cool, refreshing night air. A chorus of crickets chirped all around the yard in natural harmony. The bright stars shone brilliantly in the now clear black sky. Jule watched a satellite, barely noticeable among the stars, slowly passing over until it disappeared on the horizon. The plump full moon was just starting to reveal itself over the peak of the hill, lightly illuminating the tops of the trees below and drowning out the dimmer stars so that only the brightest remained visible. The door opened behind her, giving Jule a start. She turned around as Viktor stepped out, his phone held to his ear with his right hand.

"Hang on," he mumbled into the receiver, giving Jule an unfriendly glare. He closed the door behind him and followed the wraparound porch to the back side of the house. Though she was not normally one to spy, Jule felt compelled to investigate. She quietly sneaked along the wall of the house to get within earshot of his conversation, paying mind to keep out of sight behind the corner. Viktor's voice was barely above a whisper and Jule had difficulty hearing what he said, making out only a few words here and there.

"Azul, listen to me," Viktor said with a hiss. He mumbled again, the only words audible to Jule being "our time… coming soon… worship us…" Without hearing the other half of the conversation, Jule was left only to speculate. Fearing she may be discovered by him she decided to creep quietly back to the front of the porch. She stood back up and returned to her original position against the railing. *Azul and Viktor… what are they up to?* She wondered to herself. *It's probably nothing, I'm just being paranoid,* she shrugged off her suspicions. Jule's head began to spin again as Loki's words repeated over and over in her mind. A wave of nausea swept over her. She leaned further over the railing expecting to vomit.

The door creaked open then closed suddenly behind her, startling Jule. William walked up and leaned heavily on the railing next to her.

"Are you okay?"

Jule paused for a moment, taking in a deep breath and exhaling slowly through her nose to suppress her feeling of nausea.

"Yeah, I guess. What exactly was Loki talking about in there?" She raised an eyebrow.

William sighed heavily.

"I'm not sure if I'm the best one to explain that to you. You really should talk to Loki about it tomorrow. He didn't want to overload you with all this. That's why he wanted to introduce you to the idea today and explain more tomorrow. It'll be far less of a shock, I guess. Easier to handle in a sense?"

Jule was waiting for William to admit to the elaborate joke she thought they were playing, but he didn't. He was serious. She frowned again and looked down at the grass twinkling as it swayed in the breeze in the pale moonlight.

William turned to her.

"You trust me, don't you?"

Jule slowly nodded.

"Good." He turned his gaze to the moon, now nearly wholly visible over the hill. "Have you ever just... howled at the moon?" he asked with a grin.

Jule giggled at the ridiculous question.

"No."

"You should try it some time."

The door opened and Athan lumbered out with Esadora and Fidelia following.

"Hey, we're going to head out," Athan announced, then repeated under his breath. "Jule, if you're staying in town for a while, feel free to stop by my place." He bent down to hug her goodbye.

"Sure, of course," she replied as she exchanged hugs. "I'll see you guys around, too," she added to Esadora and Fidelia.

"I think I'm going to get out of here too," Jule said to William. "I'm uh, pretty tired." She faked a yawn.

"Alright, well it was great seeing you again. I've really missed you. Give me a call tomorrow or something. We should hang out together, like old times." He gave her a friendly smirk and a light pat on the back.

Jule stepped back inside the house to announce her departure and waved goodbye. Loki approached her and gently pulled her outside by her arm as everyone else bid her farewell.

"I'll walk you to your car," he offered and closed the door behind them.

Jule gave a quick, but meaningful hug to William before heading down the steps and brick path to her car, Loki escorting her along the way.

"Do you think you can come by tomorrow morning?" he asked.

"Sure." Jule replied mechanically.

"Well I hope you do. I have a lot to tell you and a lot to show you. Drive safe and have a good night."

Jule got in her car and Loki closed the door. She started the engine, pulled away from the curb and headed back up the hill. The drive back to Lillith's house seemed to last an eternity. Her head swirled about, her thoughts raced and she began to feel dizzy again. *I need to lie down,* she thought.

After what felt like forever, Jule finally arrived at Lillith's house. She parked her car and got out. Just as she reached the front door, her cellphone rang.

CALL FROM ANNABELLE.

Jule took a seat on the porch swing and slowly rocked back and forth. The calm breeze flowed over her as she swayed like a pendulum, the motion easing her tension.

"Hey Annabelle," she answered as she gently swung to and fro, the toes of her boots skipping across the deck.

Loud background noise and static broke through on the other end of the line.

"Hey… going… on… you… at…?"

"What? I can barely understand you. What are you doing?" Jule asked loudly into the receiver.

"Driving!" Annabelle replied.

"Why are you talking to me while you're driving?"

"…speaker phone."

"Oh, OK I guess. Why don't you call me when you have better signal? I can barely understand what you're saying."

"Can you hear me? Is that better?" Annabelle asked, finally audible.

"Yes, that's perfect. So what were you saying? Where are you going?"

"Oh, I asked what's going on and where you were at. I'm just, driving around aimlessly, killing time." Annabelle replied nonchalantly.

"I've had a really weird night," Jule confessed. "I'm back at my friend's house where I'm going to be staying. I'm pretty tired and I kind of want to go lie down."

"What do you mean you had a weird night?" Annabelle asked, concern in her voice.

"I don't think you would believe me if I told you. Hell, I barely believe it myself." Jule laughed uncomfortably. "I don't really want to talk about it right now. I just want to go to bed."

"Are you sure you don't want to talk?" Annabelle pressed on. "I'll listen, you know I'll always listen."

"I know, and yes I'm sure. Thanks. I'll talk to you later."

Jule hung up the phone and quietly opened the creaky door to Lillith's house, being mindful not to make too much noise and wake the kids. Lillith was up waiting for Jule, sitting on the couch nose-deep a book. The dogs excitedly ran up to Jule as she carefully closed the door behind her, shushing the dogs to quiet their whines.

Lillith glanced up from her book and studied Jule up and down.

"Hey, wow, you look burnt. Are you okay?" she asked as she placed her book down on the coffee table and scooted over, inviting Jule to sit on the couch next to her with a pat of her hand.

Jule plopped down heavily and let out a sigh. "I have had the weirdest night of my life." She didn't bother trying to hide anything from Lillith who could read her like a picture book.

"How so?" Lillith asked, clearly interested.

Jule reluctantly explained the odd events that took place at Loki's, which sounded even more unbelievable as she heard the words leave her lips. To her surprise, Lillith didn't treat her like she was crazy. She didn't look surprised at all. Instead, Lillith took a deep breath, turned to face Jule on the couch, and took Jule's hands in her own.

"If it was up to me, I would have told you a long time ago."

Jule jerked back her hands and her eyes widened.

"So, you're part of this?" she asked, astounded.

"Come with me outside." Lillith said as she reclaimed one of Jule's hands and led her out the back door in the kitchen.

The yard was unkempt and neglected with weeds growing all around sun-baked toys strewn about. A wobbly half-rotten wood fence crawling with vines ran along each side of the yard, leaving a gap between them at the end of a dirt path. The narrow path parted the miniature forest of wild growing weeds, reaching an abrupt drop fifteen feet in front of her to a small creek gently flowing by down below. The luminous full moon shone brightly above them making it effortless to safely navigate the yard. Never lessening her grip, Lillith took Jule down the carved path to the bank of the creek, frogs, and crickets chirping their noisy mating songs.

Lillith sat down near the water and pulled Jule down beside her. They sat in silence, listening to the enchanting music of the night.

Finally, she turned to Jule and said, "There's magick here. Can you feel it?" She paused and took a deep breath in, slowly exhaling through her nose. "Close your eyes, open your soul, and take a deep breath. In your nose and out your mouth." She demonstrated.

Jule hesitated, feeling foolish, but then followed her order. She closed her eyes and deeply breathed in the cool night air in through her nose and let the air flow heavily out of her mouth.

"Keep your eyes closed," Lillith said quietly, her voice soft and soothing. "Listen to the night, feel the energy of this place around you."

Jule recollected her brief experience in meditation, remembering to breathe deeply and slowly. She placed her hands on her knees and adjusted her position to cross her legs and straighten her back. She then focused with all her might to try and attune to her surroundings and quiet her mind. She felt a faint source of warmth slowly emanating from beneath her, growing and creeping up into her body, beginning at her toes working its way up until it tingled in her fingertips. Another wave of warmth followed and seemed to flow over her entire body back in the opposite direction. In the few times Jule had meditated, she never felt anything quite like this. Was this the "magick" Lillith was talking about? Whatever it was, Jule felt very relaxed – happy even. Her worries and doubts seemed to wash away with every wave of warmth that swept over her. Her mind was quiet and her spirit soothed.

"How do you feel?" Lillith broke the silence. "I noticed that your posture relaxed and you seem calmer now."

"I'm actually feeling a lot better," Jule said with pleasant relief. "I'm not sure what that was, but I felt *something*."

Lillith smiled. "Jule, I know what you are. I'm the one who sensed your presence and told Loki when you first arrived here. One of my abilities is that I can tell when someone like us is around. Energies are kind of my thing. That's why I'm a hermit and keep mostly to myself. I can easily get overwhelmed by other people's energies," she explained.

"OK then, what am I?" Jule speculated.

"You really want to know?"

Jule nodded.

"Well, I have spent a lot of time meditating on you, reading my cards and runes, and I truly believe that you are a lycanthrope – a werewolf."

Jule couldn't help but laugh. This was ridiculous to her and she couldn't believe that Lillith, of all people, was playing at her like this. But, would Lillith really do that? The rational part of Jule kept her skeptical, while another part of her wanted so much to believe that there was something more than just mundane life; it wanted to believe in the mythical world. She found her grounded-self in a split conflict.

"How am I a werewolf? I've never turned into a wolf in all the full moons I've experienced and I've certainly never run around on all fours like a dog," Jule argued, still skeptical.

"Ah, well that's the interesting part." Lillith smiled. "Every person is different, every species and ability gets activated a different way. Some, like me, are born with it. We know from birth who and what we are and have that advantage to practice and perfect our talents over time throughout our whole life. Others, like you, contain something in your DNA that needs to be awakened, in a sense. Only then will you be able to be who you truly are. Some unfortunates, however, never activate their gene and never know anything beyond their limited human life. I pity them."

"OK, so how do I trigger my gene?" Jule was now intrigued, her curiosity and excitement rising.

"That's what you need to go talk to Loki about. He can guide you down that path better than I can."

"So, what are your abilities? What are you?"

"You know what I am! I'm a witch! My 'species' and abilities are more socially acceptable, so I don't have to try very hard to blend in or hide who I am. Once in a while though I come across an ignorant person who sees my jewelry or tattoos and calls me a Satanist." Lillith rolled her eyes. "I used to try to educate them and remind them that Satan is part of the *Christian* religion, not Pagan, but I've given up," she scoffed. "Witches are everywhere, some have abilities like I do and others simply practice the Pagan way of life, whichever path that may be. Being an empath my abilities revolve around emotions and energies. I can feel what others are feeling around me as if they were my emotions, and I can sense people around me through their energy. I can tell if someone is trustworthy as soon as I meet them, I can tell if someone has negative intentions, and I can tell if there's more to someone than meets the eye. I'm like an energy and emotional sponge, and it can be incredibly overwhelming sometimes. I also have a talent for divination, but you knew that already, too."

"Interesting," was all Jule could muster up to say, though it all strangely made sense. Lillith always had this crazy talent for knowing exactly *how* Jule was feeling and somehow always knew what to do to make her feel better. They both sat in silence a while longer by the creek, then they both stood up together and returned to the house.

"I'm going to bed. I'll see you in the morning." Jule said with a yawn and hugged Lillith goodnight. She went into the guest house, kicked off her shoes and plopped down on the bed, her head sinking into the soft pillows. Sleep found Jule easily that night as she drifted effortlessly off, welcoming her dreams of incredible possibilities.

MORE THAN HUMAN

CHAPTER 4

The morning sun peered blindingly through the window onto Jule's face. She stirred awake, then groggily climbed out of bed and got herself together. The warm and delightful smell of coffee greeted Jule as she entered Lillith's house. Lillith was scrambling about the kitchen, holding her baby in one arm, stirring the eggs and flipping the bacon she was cooking with the other arm, all the while shooing the dog back with her leg.

"Do you need any help?" Jule offered as she laughed at the humorous scene she stumbled into.

"Nah, I'm a strong, independent woman. I do this every day, I got this!" she proudly exclaimed. "Get yourself some coffee and have a seat. I hope you're hungry."

Jule helped herself and sat at the kitchen table next to Lillith's oldest daughter who was scribbling away on some blank paper with crayons.

"Hi, Auntie Jule," Xena tiredly mumbled as she rubbed her eyes.

"Good morning sweetie," Jule said softly, giving her a light pat on the head. "What are you drawing?"

"I dunno," Xena mumbled again as she continued her colorful scribbles.

She's so cute, Jule thought to herself.

Lillith finished preparing breakfast and placed Abigail in the play pen. Jule sipped on her coffee, feeling no appetite, merely picking at her food.

"Not hungry?" Lillith asked disappointed.

Jule shook her head.

"That's OK, the dogs can eat it. I know you never eat much in the mornings, but I thought I would offer." Lillith smiled and continued eating her meal.

Jule finished her coffee and rinsed her cup out in the sink.

"I'm going over to Loki's now."

"Oh okay, good! Well, good luck," Lillith replied as she stood up to walk Jule out the door.

Jule got in her car, waved goodbye, and started towards Loki's, unsure of what to expect.

When she arrived she noticed a small red pick-up truck parked outside on the curb. *William is here.* Jule's stomach fluttered, anxious to see him again. As she followed the brick path to the house, she noticed him standing at the top of the stairs, apparently waiting for her. Seeing him immediately comforted her and lifted her spirits. He smiled cheerfully as she approached and extended his arms inviting an embrace. Jule gave him a quick, tight hug and stepped back. The door opened and Loki invited them both inside.

Jule took a seat in the living room on the large couch she occupied the night before and William sat next to her, keeping a small, intentional space between them. Loki took a seat in a chair opposite them.

"Would you like any coffee?" Loki offered, beginning to stand up.

"No thanks, I've already had some."

"I'd like a cup." William perked up. "But I'll just get it myself." He signaled Loki to remain seated and disappeared into the kitchen.

Jule's anxiety started up again as Loki stared at her. He leaned back in his chair and crossed his legs. He rested his elbows on the arms of the chair and folded his hands in front of his face, pressing his two index fingers together against his lips. Jule fidgeted in her seat. She didn't enjoy the feeling of being put on the spot. William returned and sat back down next to Jule, placing his coffee on the table in front of him and resting back casually.

"Jule, I invited William here to join us because I thought his presence would help make you feel more at ease. I know how close you two are."

Jule nodded and William smirked at her, giving her a playful nudge with his elbow. Her stomach fluttered again.

"I'm sure you have many questions, but I would like to try to explain things first," Loki began. "As I said last night, we are not human and neither are you. Our bodies may resemble that of humans, but it's not our bodies that define us and who we are. Our core, our souls, our *spirits* are that of our 'other being' – who we were throughout our past lives. Our 'True Self'. You are familiar with the concept of reincarnation, yes?"

Jule nodded. "Yes, I know a little about it. Basically, when you die just your body dies and your spirit comes back in another form to live another life. It's a repeated cycle. That's about all I know."

"Correct!" Loki confirmed. "Reincarnation, however, is different depending on the species. I, for example, *am* Loki."

"The Norse god from mythology?"

"Yup," Loki replied.

"Bullshit." Jule scoffed at his confirmation. *A god, really*? This was the most absurd thing he had said so far. Loki shot her a wounded glance, all pleasantness removed from his face. Jule's eyes dropped to the floor in shame of insulting her friend. Suppressing her doubts for now, she politely waited for Loki to continue.

"For me, I reincarnate at different levels. My reincarnation process is dictated by my behavior in each life. Since, as you may know, I have a reputation of being fairly naughty as a god, a few hundred years back I was demoted to the status of human by the other gods, which *could* have been a much worse punishment, if I'm being honest. At least I wasn't demoted down to a cockroach or something," he chuckled. "Now I live each life as a human until I am considered 'worthy' of returning to my god status. Then, I can have a lot of fun again." He smiled devilishly.

"OK…" Jule said. "So, is Bradley actually Thor or something?" Her tone was a little more smug than she intended, but Loki seemed to ignore it.

"No, no," he laughed. "Just because Bradley is my brother in this life does not mean he is my god-brother. We share mortal blood, that is all, but he is still no less of a brother to me." Loki paused for a moment before continuing. "So my point about reincarnation is to connect it with the idea of being *immortal*. Our souls, who we are, continue to exist and pass on through different lives. Sometimes we can recall our past life experiences and know, based on that, exactly who we are, and sometimes we cannot. But, regardless of if you know who you really are or not, in order to be your True Self, your particular dormant species gene has to be activated."

Jule recalled her conversation with Lillith by the stream the previous night.

"Yeah, Lillith mentioned something like that to me. She told me that some have their gene already activated, some need to activate it, and others are never able to."

"Correct," Loki confirmed. "Did she tell you what we think you are?"

"She said I was a lycanthrope," she answered, embarrassed at her own words.

"Yes, that is the conclusion we have come to. Lillith is incredibly talented at detecting other beings like us and identifying what they are through her art of divination. She's certain that's what you are. William here seems to agree with her." Loki nodded towards William.

"OK…" Jule said with uncertainty. "So, you've told me what I supposedly am, what are the rest of you?"

"Well we covered me," Loki began. "William here is also a lycanthrope."

William smiled a toothy, irresistible grin.

"Don't worry, I won't bite, unless you want me to," he said in jest with a wink. Jule blushed as she momentarily fantasized about William nibbling on her neck.

"As for the others," Loki continued. "Athan is beginning to master his abilities as a witch; his didn't come as naturally to him as it does for others."

"Don't you mean he's a *warlock*?" Jule interrupted.

"No, and don't you ever call him that to his face," Loki said completely serious. "He is a witch. A witch is a witch, whether the person is male or female. The term 'warlock' is a derogatory term for a witch that has done something wrong and been ostracized by their coven. It's an insult. Some male witches out there are trying to reclaim the term, but Athan is one of those who is offended by it."

"Oh, wow. I didn't realize that there was a difference," Jule muttered, embarrassed at making offense yet again. "I apologize for my ignorance."

"It's perfectly alright," Loki assured her. "It's really not common knowledge. In addition to being a witch, Athan is also sort of our own personal history keeper. He collects old books, maps, legends, family trees, anything he can get his hands on. Rayme is our shaman; he is human but has a unique talent in herbal remedies and medicines specifically for the treatment of each species. He's absolutely amazing at it, too. We're lucky to have someone like him around. Demonik is a vampire, Catarina is a succubus, Esadora is a seer tapping into a new concept for her called 'spirit immersion', Fidelia is a type of nymph that shape-shifts into a cat, Azul is a dragon, and Viktor is a demon."

"I could have called that last one," Jule joked. "What is 'spirit immersion'?"

"Esadora has the ability to transfer her spirit, or life force, directly to another. All she has to do is concentrate on a specific person and her spirit basically leaves her body and immediately enters that of the subject. As of now, she can only simply inhabit their body, not control it. She can hear, smell, feel, taste, and see anything that whoever she immerses with is experiencing at that moment, for as long as she inhabits them. I believe that with more training she could be a very powerful individual, perhaps completely taking over another person and having full control of them."

"Well that's pretty cool." *And kind of scary…*

"There are others out there, all different kinds of species and abilities," Loki added. "Many seem to gravitate to this area for some reason. Something about this place draws other beings here, though I'm not exactly sure why." Loki paused for a moment in speculation. "Becoming your True Self is a wonderful gift that not all are given. A lot of other beings never realize who and what they truly are, never knowing what they're really capable of. For example, some marine biologist who feels the irresistible pull of the ocean may never realize that he or she is actually, truly, a mermaid. The pilot who feels most at home in the skies may never experience their own pair of wings that are waiting to emerge and carry them, soaring through the clouds. The professional equestrian rider who feels at-one with their horse may never know that deep down they're truly a centaur, all because the dormant gene can be so unpredictable that some are never able activate it. It's unfortunate."

"So I'm supposed to believe that you are a god," Jule said to Loki, then turned to William. "– that you are a werewolf, and that there are nymphs and demons and vampires all about?"

"I know you're hesitant to believe it, but we will show you." William said.

"What about Bradley? You never mentioned what Bradley is supposed to be."

"We haven't been able to pinpoint exactly what species he is. He hasn't exhibited any signs so far and Lillith can't get a reading on him, so we don't know." Loki replied rather disappointed, his eyes wandering.

"You mentioned some sort of religious group, the Order of Purity?"

Loki snapped back. "Oh yes. You need to know more about them as well." He took a deep breath before continuing. "The Order of Purity is an ancient religious sect, a branch of the Catholic Church actually, that stemmed from the radical teachings of a self-proclaimed Italian prophet named Melkior Lavenchii. He taught about conquering demons while claiming that he spoke to God and was warned about the evils that plagued mankind and that God Himself was using Melkior as his personal assassin. Many sheep followed his ways and as is true with most religions, his teachings were bastardized and molded into the ideology that the Order follows today, bent and contorted to fit their own distorted beliefs. They've existed for hundreds of years, hunting down other beings. They believe we are filth, a creation of the devil, and must be eliminated. They keep secret records of families who have been proven 'guilty' and use the ancestry as a guide for monitoring future 'threats'. The Order is very cunning. If they suspect an individual of being of another species, they will often plant an agent in the area to blend in whilst stalking the individual, always watching for signs of their target's True Self and learning everything they can about their target. They hide in plain sight, which is why we have to be cautious."

Jule nodded.

"Now, are you prepared to become your True Self?" Loki asked Jule.

Jule looked up at Loki and then glanced at William who simply smiled back at her with his soft eyes. She turned back to Loki and took a deep breath.

"I guess so," she said. "You've certainly piqued my curiosity. So what do I do next? Does William have to bite me or something?" She turned to William who shot her a mischievous look.

Loki let out a chuckle. "No that's not how it works. You're already a lycan, your gene is simply dormant right now and we need to wake it up." He clapped his hands and rubbed them together.

"How do we do that?"

"I wish I had a straight answer for you," Loki said with a grimace. "But since it's different for everyone, we'll have to try a few things. First,

Fidelia is going to take you to a woman who lives in a remote cabin in the wilderness. After your visit with her, we will see what we need to do next."

"Who is this woman?"

"Her name is Rose. She is old and wise, another like us, who lives by herself, isolated and away from town. She has a very unique ability that I think will help you the most. She's a sort of witch, I guess you could call her. Rose is a very… interesting woman with very little social skills, so you may find her to be a bit eccentric."

"OK, when is this happening?"

Loki looked down at his watch. "She should be arriving within the hour to pick you up."

Jule was surprised at how quickly this was happening, rushing into this world of mystery and fantasy, but it was thrilling at the same time. She had always been fascinated by mythological creatures, reading all about them in her spare time, and was drawn to werewolves in particular ever since she could remember. She was enthralled that she could actually *be* one of these monstrous creatures she secretly coveted.

MORE THAN HUMAN

CHAPTER 5

Fidelia alerted them of her arrival by a brief honk of her horn from outside.

"I guess that's for me," Jule said as she stood up and said her goodbyes.

"Good luck," Loki wished her as they parted ways.

Jule got into Fidelia's Jeep and they were off.

"Rose lives pretty far out of town, so it will take us about an hour to get there," Fidelia informed Jule.

"Cool. Hey, do you mind if I smoke? I know you don't…" Jule politely asked.

"Sure, I don't mind. Just roll your window down."

Jule obliged, rolling the window down all the way and lit a cigarette, taking a deep drag and puffing the smoke out. They sat in silence for a while as she enjoyed the scenery of the juniper-covered rolling hills and the fresh mountain air blowing through her hair. Climbing in elevation, they began leaving the juniper behind in exchange for tall black pines and giant red ponderosas. The temperature began to drop as they ascended the windy mountain road to their destination.

"I feel like I don't really know any of you anymore," Jule admitted.

Fidelia frowned. "What do you mean?"

Jule took a deep sigh and explained, "No one is what I thought they were. You are all... *I* am not human? You guys have all had this huge secret and just decided to tell me now, years after I've known you?"

Fidelia seemed to be at a loss for words, keeping her eyes focused on the road in front of her.

"And why tell me this now," Jule continued. "Why not before? Why tell me at all?"

"We decided to tell you now because we may need you. I know that sounds selfish, but it's true. Loki and I have noticed a potential problem with a few of the more unruly members of the group and with your association to us the Order may try to come after you. We need you to help us, and we want to help protect you."

"Let me guess: Viktor and Azul are the problematic ones."

"Yes, how did you know?" she asked, sarcastically.

"They both seem so unpredictable, which also makes them dangerous."

"That's quite an astute and accurate observation. Those two are loose cannons. Viktor with his drinking and Azul with his irrational and emotional outbursts. Neither one of them is rational, come to think of it. They're both entirely driven by testosterone."

"Last night, I heard Viktor on the phone with Azul." Jule confessed.

"Oh?"

"I couldn't hear much other than 'our time, coming soon, worship us'. What do you suppose that means?"

Fidelia's eyebrows furrowed.

"I'm not sure, but that's probably something you should tell Loki."

The girls sat in silence for a few moments, tension and worry filling the air. Jule fidgeted absentmindedly with her hands in her lap as she stared out the window hypnotized by the passing trees.

"So, why do you need me? What can I do?" She broke the silence.

"When you become your True Self you will be a force to be reckoned with, Jule. Lycans are very powerful creatures. If Viktor and Azul were to lose it, having two lycans would be a great advantage."

"Well, what if you're wrong? What if I am just a human?"

"I strongly believe you are a lycanthrope, Jule. I've met a few and your human personality definitely points to it. You're methodical and level-headed. You're honest and deeply loyal. You're brave and just, but you're also containing a fiery rage inside you that's itching to be unleashed. I can see it."

Jule became a little embarrassed. She worked very hard on controlling her anger and thought she was doing a good job at it, but now she doubted herself. *A fiery rage inside, itching to be unleashed.* She never looked at it that way before. Her whole life she has struggled to keep her emotions in check, her angry outbursts being the most difficult to control, but over time and with practice she made progress.

"Yeah, I guess I do," Jule somewhat shamefully agreed. She began to imagine what it would be like to be a werewolf, to be such an awesome and fearsome creature. She fantasized about the potential of strength, speed, and the exhilarating freedom to be wild, and she smiled.

"So, tell me about you then. What's your species?" Jule inquired.

"I am a cat sith; a type of nymph that relates mostly to the feline species. We originate from Scotland and Ireland, my family being from Ireland," Fidelia responded with pride.

"Do you have any special abilities?"

Fidelia chuckled. "I can transform into a large black cat and I'm very nature oriented, but that's about it, nothing too fancy. My cousin, however, can transform into a big black cat with wings!."

"That's pretty neat, actually," Jule said, impressed. "Loki mentioned there were other species out there. Do you know any others?"

Fidelia smiled. "I sure do!" she exclaimed. "Have you ever heard of a selkie?"

Jule shook her head.

"A really close friend of mine who lives in Oregon is a selkie. Basically, she can shapeshift from a beautiful woman – and she is gorgeous, I might add – into a seal, so naturally she lives near the ocean."

"That's cool," Jule remarked. "What about this Rose lady, what is she? All Loki said was you could classify her as a witch…"

"Rose has a very unique ability, which is why Loki is sending you to her. She is also very particular about the people who can go and see her, so that's why I'm taking you instead of him," she explained. "Rose has the ability to transform any living being into another. So the goal is: Rose will help you experience your first transformation into your True Self so you will know how it feels and what to expect when you try to achieve transformation on your own."

"She's going to what!?" Jule exclaimed, eyes wide with surprise.

"It's okay. I'll be there," she coaxed. "Nothing bad will happen to you, I promise. Rose knows what she is doing."

Jule stared out the window, her anxiety pulsing through her body.

"We're here," Fidelia announced as she pulled onto a long dirt driveway tucked away beneath the trees. The clearing revealed a quaint little cottage on the top of a hill.

"That's where we're going?"

"Yup, neat little place, isn't it?"

"It's cute."

She examined the property as they drove closer. Blooming roses, zinnia, poppies, hollyhocks, and cosmos of all colors imaginable hugged the side of the log house giving it a most beautiful floral natural decoration. Ferns, ivy, and coleus crept along the ground between the flowers. Herbs of all kinds occupied a small square garden just to the right of the home, all in bloom, with bees buzzing busily about them. Jule could swear that she saw a few cannabis plants cleverly hidden among the jungle. *Neat old lady.*

As Fidelia parked her vehicle, an enormous gray and white wolf came trotting from behind the old vine-covered cabin to greet them. The wolf's fur shone brilliantly with a strange blueish hue in the sunlight giving him a magical glow. His magnificent golden eyes captivated Jule as she stepped out of the vehicle. He paused a few feet from her, standing tall and confident, staring her down. She failed his challenge as his sharp, intimidating gaze forced her eyes down, giving the wolf his due respect and ultimately submitting to him.

"Kami!" Fidelia squealed with delight as the giant wolf turned his intense gaze from Jule and happily loped up to her. Nearly knocking her over with his great size, the massive animal stood up on his hind legs and smothered Fidelia with licks. He stood a full head-and-a-half taller than Fidelia and his paws dwarfed her hands. He got down from his greeting and trotted over to investigate Jule, carefully sniffing her from head to toe, his tail still as he decided whether to permit Jule to enter his territory. Jule stood unmoved, keeping calm in his strong presence. She allowed him to go about his business, offering him her hand with her palm facing down. He took a deep inhale of her hand before sneezing it out and proceeded to wag his tail. She was accepted. Jule gladly stroked his thick, soft fur around his head as he gave her slobbery licks of approval.

"Fidelia, you're here!" a voice called from inside the cabin. Jule stood up and her eyes fell upon a frail elderly Asian woman, slightly

46

hunched over in the doorway. She smiled sweetly and gave a brief welcoming wave.

"Hi Rose! Yes, we're here. Sorry if we're a little late. This is Jule," Fidelia said. Jule extended her hand in greeting to the old woman.

Rose firmly took Jule's hand and looked her hard in the eye, the old woman's black eyes stern and unnerving.

"Let me get a look at you," she said as she released Jule's hand and began slowly circling around her, scanning her up and down. She stopped in front of Jule, demanding her hand again. Jule glanced at Fidelia who simply nodded back at her. She reluctantly offered the old woman her hand. Rose quickly snatched it up in her own wrinkled, frail hand and turned it over so that her palm was facing up. The old woman studied Jule's palm markings carefully, making odd noises to herself and nodding her head. She looked deep into Jule's eyes and smiled, gently releasing her.

"Come inside you two," she ordered. She turned to the open door and lead the girls in. "Kami, you stay outside and guard."

The wolf whined in protest and turned around, plopping down on a sunny patch of grass. His ears were erect and alert as he stared down the road.

"Please, make yourselves comfortable dears." Rose slowly shifted her way through the home towards the kitchen.

Jule looked around the cabin at the beautiful oriental decorum. All kinds of bonsai trees of different shapes, sizes, and species were placed all over, their soil decorated with gleaming gemstones and sparkling crystals. Ornate rugs were hung on the walls with golden threads of dragons soaring over mountains and cherry-blossomed trees. One tapestry in particular caught her attention: a plain roll of white fabric hanging on a brass rod encased behind glass and iron bars. If the iron bars weren't enough, a heavy chain with an ancient-looking padlock sealed the display case securely. A label with the faded words "Ittan-Momen" was plastered on the bottom framework of the display. As she continued taking her personal tour of the cabin, Jule swore she saw the strange tapestry move inside the case. Her eyes fixated on the cloth, waiting to witness it shift about on its own, but it remained still. *Just a piece of cloth strangely locked on the wall.* The cabin itself was made of a dark red wood that may have been cherry wood but Jule wasn't sure and she didn't bother to ask. She admired the plethora of dragon decorations, with their long flowing mustaches and snake-like bodies, each brightly colored with reds, oranges, and golds. Tapestries of dragons hung in every window.

Near the kitchen on the floor was a large bronze statue of what Jule assumed was Buddha. A matching bronze tray lay at the crossed legs of the Buddha generously adorned with flowers and herbs. Several cats were running about the home playfully chasing each other around, darting this way and that.

Fidelia led Jule through a doorway of dangling red beads to a large table near the back of the home. An old iron chandelier with lit candles hung above it being the only source of light in the room. No windows or natural light of any kind entered here. Jule noticed that there weren't nearly as many decorations in this part of the cabin either. Instead, a lone altar with another ornate gold and purple cloth draped over it and incense burning in a silver dragon burner occupied the far corner. The air was still and the smoke from the incense gently floated upwards in a steady stream, uninterrupted by drafts. She found the smoke to be hypnotizing and didn't notice when Rose quietly entered the room and placed an oriental tea set on the table next to her.

"Tea?" she offered.

Jule snapped back to reality from her entranced moment. "Oh, yes please," she said, not wanting to be rude and deny the woman her offering.

Rose smiled, pouring a small cup of tea for them and took a seat. She studied Jule intensely, making her feel a little uncomfortable.

"I am Rose," the old woman began. "But you can call me Sama. We will get straight to the point. Do you know what I do?"

"Well, kind of," Jule began. "You can turn any living thing into another, right?"

Sama nodded.

"And do you know why *you* are here?" the old woman asked.

"No, I don't," Jule lied. She knew full well why she was there, but deep down she needed to hear it from the old woman herself.

Fidelia shot her a disapproving look, clearly unhappy with Jule's attempt at playing dumb.

"You are here so I can help you transform into your True Self for the first time. After I force you to go through the change, it should be easier for you to change on your own. Or, at least that is the idea."

Jule swallowed a gulp of tea down hard. This woman was going to turn her into a werewolf. Her anxiety began to kick in again, her fight-or-flight instinct taking affect. Her eyes darted towards the front door for a fast escape, then she turned and met Fidelia's gaze. Sensing her discomfort, Fidelia gently placed a hand over hers. Jule began to calm down, reaching for her cup and finishing her tea.

"More?" Sama offered.

"Please," Jule said as she held out her cup.

"You seem a bit… unconvinced –skeptical. Would you like a demonstration of my ability?" Sama questioned.

Jule didn't know what to say. She glanced over at Fidelia who was smirking. Jule turned back to Sama who quickly snatched up a black cat running by in her arms and cradled it upside-down. The cat fought her grasp and frantically struggled, desperately trying to free itself from her clutches. She held him down firmly as she rocked it back and forth, slowly swinging her body in rhythmical motion. As she cradled the cat, its fidgeting slowed and he began to go limp, his eyes lulled and relaxed, almost as if he was falling into a trance. She continued rocking the cat, back and forth, whispering incoherently into its ear. Jule's eyes widened in amazement as the cat's green eyes began to glow. It was dim at first, but then grew to illuminate the entire room, giving an eerie ambiance. The cat began to make an awful, drawn-out meow as fur began falling off in clumps and collecting on the floor beneath them. Its skin started changing from its black coloration into a light naked pink. His tail shriveled up and withered away, plopping onto the floor like a shriveled-up umbilical cord. The creature began wiggling again in the old woman's arms as she held it tightly against her chest and covered it with her shawl, quickly turning away. The cat's meow began distorting, sounding less like a cat and more like the cry of a baby. Sama turned around to face Jule, gently pulling away the shawl and revealing the being that occupied her arms. The cat that Jule had seen the woman pick up just a moment ago was no longer. The woman now held a human baby, peacefully sleeping in her arms.

Jule stared in awe. She couldn't believe her eyes. Fidelia simply grinned as she sipped her tea in amusement.

MORE THAN HUMAN

CHAPTER 6

The old woman returned the unnatural infant into its original feline form. The cat briskly leapt out of her arms onto the floor, giving a most disgruntled look before darting off.

"You're lucky that it's a full moon," Sama said. "Otherwise this experience would be extremely unpleasant for you." She slowly began sifting through a small wardrobe opposite the table, collecting a few items awkwardly in her arms and preparing for her task. Fidelia rushed to help her as she struggled to retrieve a blanket from the top shelf that was too high for her to reach.

"Ah, thank you dear, such a good kitty you are," her wrinkled face grinned wide as she patted Fidelia gently on the head.

Fidelia smirked facetiously.

"Do you need any help setting up? Can I do anything?" she politely offered.

"Fetch some more hot water; we're going to need more tea."

"Yes, Sama." Fidelia respectfully bowed before the old woman and quickly darted off into the kitchen as she was ordered.

"Should I be doing anything?" Jule asked nervously feeling useless.

"No, no. You just relax and drink. Do you like pipe tobacco?"

"Oh, no thank you."

As she drank more of her odd yet delicious jasmine tea, Jule began feeling a tingling sensation creeping throughout her body. Her head started to feel loopy and her ears began to ring.

"What's in this tea?" she managed to ask, her speech slurred.

"I added a special herb that will ease your transformation, but it may make you feel a little funny. I didn't think you would drink it if you knew. Don't worry, it's harmless. The effects will wear off in a few hours. Just relax and don't fight it."

Sama laid out a blanket. Disoriented, Jule stumbled to the floor.

"Now, Jule, I need you to remove all of your clothes and place them on the table; you don't want to ruin them during your change."

Sama helped Jule to her feet and she reluctantly began removing her clothes, embarrassed to be completely nude in front of a stranger, and placed them on the table. She stood awkwardly in front of the woman, timidly covering her bare breasts with her crossed arms.

"Here," she directed as she helped Jule lie down. "We need to wait a few minutes for your body to completely absorb what I have given you. Now, tell me what you know about lycans – werewolves."

"Well what I know from movies and books is that they transform during full moons, are wild, rabid beasts, and silver is deadly to them," Jule said. "Especially silver bullets."

Sama laughed. "There's some truth to what you say. After all, every mythology holds some bit of truth to it. The full moon's energy allows for a smoother transformation and with some practice the change will come naturally – effortlessly to you. The moon doesn't *force* a transformation, however. Lycans aren't mindless, bloodthirsty beasts, either. You are still you. Every feeling and emotion you have remains, they just inhabit a different body." Sama sat down at Jule's side with a groan as her frail body protested the descent. "Now, silver is dangerous to lycans if it is in an open wound. The metal prevents the lycan's ability to regenerate and quickly heal, so the risk of bleeding to death from a minor wound is very high if the wound was inflicted by a silver weapon. Silver bullets, if struck in the right spot, will kill anyone. It's a bullet."

Jule nodded her head, the room still spinning about her. Sweat began to drip from her temples down the sides of her face. Waves of heat and prickling stings crawled across her body. Fidelia rushed back in, setting the tray of freshly-brewed tea carefully on the table.

"Here, to make you more comfortable," Sama said as she draped a large, heavy oriental cloth over Jule .

"Have you started yet?" Fidelia asked.

"Yes, we have." Sama confirmed as she looked down at Jule. "Jule, whether you are ready or not, your transformation will now begin; take a deep breath and close your eyes."

Jule obeyed as the old woman crouched over on her knees with her hands hovering just above Jule's body. Fidelia moved to the side, keeping out of the way. Sama began softly mumbling the incoherent commands she had used on the cat. Jule thought Sama was speaking in a different language. Japanese perhaps? The woman's voice began to echo in Jule's ears, her skin itching uncomfortably. Sama continued her chants, echoing louder and louder in Jule's head. The itching grew into burning and Jule involuntarily let out a moan of pain as she writhed on the floor.

"It's okay Jule, I'm here. Just try to relax," Fidelia gently coaxed.

Jule's body began sweating uncontrollably, her muscles tensing and contorting, her bones stretching and bending unnaturally. She felt a jolt of electricity shoot through her gut, forcing her to roll over onto all fours, the blanket sliding off her. Thick light brown fur quickly began spreading, covering her whole body as her jaw painfully extended and narrowed displaying her new vicious canine teeth. Blood dripped from her mouth as she accidentally bit her tongue, dangling out the side of her jowls. Her round human ears elongated to furry points, now more sensitive to sound than ever. Her shoulders tightened and her spine straightened as a narrow tail began to protrude out the base of her back. Her legs lengthened and shifted taking their new shape, her hips displacing and readjusting. Her outstretched arms extended, her fingers shrinking and melding into paws armed with enormous sharp claws. Jule's moans of pain were now howls of distress as she no longer had the capacity for human voice. As quickly as the change began, it was over. The pain and discomfort subsided as Jule, now a great wolf, stood in the middle of the room on all fours panting heavily, her legs shaking awkwardly like a newborn calf. Her once gray-blue eyes now shone with a magnificent deep yellow. The dimness of the room no longer inhibited her ability to see; she now had perfect, enhanced vision.

"Now, dear, experience what it is to *be* a lycan," Sama said as she signaled Jule to follow her outside.

On strange and new wobbly limbs Jule approached the doorway, stopping at the threshold, raising her head high and pointed her ears forward. Kami quickly rose from his resting place and playfully approached the new form of Jule. Her enhanced vision allowed her to see

Kami as he truly was –a wolf made of blue lightning. Jule recalled a lesson she had in Japanese mythology and identified him as a Raiju. He was even more magnificent now that she could see his pure form with her true eyes.

"Go, Jule, go and feel your new power."

As soon as she stepped beyond the threshold of the door Jule felt the forest calling to her, beckoning her. She flexed her new bear-sized paws, digging her large razor-sharp claws into the ground, shifting the dirt beneath her. She raised her snout to the wind and inhaled deeply, sniffing her surroundings, identifying each smell. The scent of the water in the lake a mile away floated softly in the breeze and the perfume of freshly-cut hay fields rose into her snout. The hard hooves of grazing deer striking the rocks as they walked in the distance thudded in her ears. Her enhanced senses excited her, giving her a tingle down her spine to the tip of her tail. She wagged her new appendage enthusiastically. She now yearned to put her physical form and abilities to the test. Bracing herself backwards she took a mighty leap forward and began running with all her soul and might, her paws pounding the ground beneath her. She tore through the woods, effortlessly winding between trees and leaping over fallen logs with agility and ease. Every muscle fiber and sinew was charged with power. She felt free, she felt alive, and she felt wild. Her heart pounded in her chest, her muscles burning with every stride, but still she kept on, too enthralled with this new feeling to pay any mind.

Kami fast approached as he chased her through the woods, giving her a beast of similar proportions to compete with. Addicted to her newfound power she forgot every danger that lurked, every worry she had, and gleefully played with her wolf-kin. She watched as Kami approached a tree, stood up on his hind legs and scratched some bark off, making a scar on the trunk. Jule imitated him and found that standing on her hind legs felt as natural as running on all fours. She reached her mighty paws up as far as she could and dragged her claws down the tree, scarring it deeply. Taking a step back she was able to compare the height of the marks, finding that hers greatly exceeded those of Kami's, which she estimated were easily six feet high. Being petite all her life she was impressed by her new gargantuan size. How intimidating she must be now!

The two wolves caught a strange scent carried on the wind and took off again at full speed, instinct taking over. Suddenly Kami abruptly halted in a clearing, turning his head back toward the direction of the cabin with his ears forward and alert. Jule stopped beside him and listened. In the distance, she heard the voice of Sama calling them back. Both wolves tore off chasing each other back to the cabin.

"Jule, we need to change you back," Sama said as the beasts approached. "Kami, you stay outside."

The old woman led the brown wolf into her home to the back room. On the floor, Jule noticed a bowl filled with some kind of liquid. She sniffed at it and grimaced at the foul-smelling substance.

"There's more tea for you to drink to aid your transformation. Get to it," Sama commanded as she pointed to the bowl.

Parched from her run and panting heavily Jule greedily lapped up the contents, ignoring the off-putting aroma.

"Now, lie down."

Fidelia chuckled at Sama's command.

Jule obeyed as Sama knelt beside her and performed her ritual once again. The transformation back to a human wasn't nearly as painful or excruciating as the change into a wolf, Jule noticed. Returned to her human self, Jule collected her clothes and got dressed, still shaking from the adrenaline rush.

"Sit down for a moment, there's more I need to tell you," Sama ordered.

Jule took a seat at the table. She felt so weak now, so sluggish, blind and deaf compared to her other self that she experienced. Jule never noticed that she felt like something was missing from her identity – never knowing who she truly was. Now that she had been exposed to this other side of herself she felt complete, satisfied and proud. She had a new glow about her, a new confidence she hadn't displayed before, an entirely new sense of herself.

"I must warn you," Sama began, concerned. "Do you know how long you were out there?"

Jule shook her head. She was so involved and occupied by her excitement that time didn't matter to her.

"You were in your wolf form for over five hours."

"What?" she exclaimed, "It couldn't have been that long. I swear it only felt like twenty minutes."

"You need to pay attention to the time that passes when you are in your wolf form. If you stay a wolf for too long, you will not be able to change back. Any more than a day is a risk. You will lose all of who you are," Sama warned. "You will become a mindless, dangerous beast. Do you understand?"

Jule nodded. *Well that sucks,* she thought.

"I have shown you what it feels like to change. Now you must learn, on your own, the ability to change yourself. I am of no further help to you and I've done all that I can. I wish you luck in your journey." Sama escorted the girls out of her home. Jule made sure to give ample appreciation and a respectful bow before getting in the car and returning to Loki's.

CHAPTER 7

Loki and William were waiting outside for Jule and Fidelia to return. Jule's legs felt shaky and weak as she walked up the stairs, hanging onto the railing for support. William moved towards her and offered his arm, smiling brightly. Jule gratefully accepted, abandoning the railing in exchange for the support of his arm. They made their way into the house and he assisted Jule to the couch, taking a seat next to her once again. Fidelia plopped herself down on the floor to the side of the coffee table. Jule hesitated to release her grasp of William's hand, but did so as Loki took a seat in a chair across from them.

"So, tell me how it went," Loki asked interested.

"It was awesome." Jule grinned from ear to ear. "I felt so strong, so free, so *wild*. It was exhilarating! The most amazing experience of my life!"

"Isn't it?" William said, his eyes gleaming.

"Good, so Rose was able to help you change?" Loki returned to the point.

"Yes, she did," Jule confirmed. "She also said that she's of 'no further help to' me."

Loki nodded. "Yes, that is the extent of her power. She can change you herself but you need to learn how to achieve a transformation on your own. Now –" he said quietly. "—that is where I come in."

"Oh?" Jule asked with a raised eyebrow.

"This is the not-so-fun part," Loki admitted with a frown as he stood up and began to pace the room, crossing his hands behind his back as he moved about. "Since the trigger is different for everyone, we will have to subject you to different tests. We will begin with the easiest and then progress to more difficult and trying tests. I may have to put you through some pretty harsh situations. We need to stress your body and your mind out to the point where it triggers your lycan gene, so you may have full control over your ability." Loki paused for a moment. "Now, remember Jule: I am your friend. I am not doing this to hurt you in any way; I'm doing this to *help* you." Loki stopped in front of her and placed his hands reassuringly on Jule's shoulders as he said this, apology written in his eyes.

Jule nodded but remained silent. William reached out to hold her hand in comfort, assuring her that everything would be fine. Fidelia patted Jule gently on the knee in a "good luck" sort of way.

"What's going to be the first test, then?" she finally asked.

"You're coming home with me," William smirked. "We're going to see if Rose's forced transformation triggered you or not… to see if you can just will yourself to change on your own. It's easier performed under the full moon, and tonight being the second night of the full moon makes it perfect. The power of the moon is always strongest on the second day of the full phase. You'll have a better chance of transforming on your own tonight, if you can at all."

Jule immediately blushed. The thought of spending the night *alone* with William excited her. Loki noticed the increase in chemistry between them and grinned.

"I'm sorry guys, I've got to run," Fidelia announced suddenly as she stood up and headed for the door, waving goodbye.

"Hey, where's Bradley?" Jule asked when she finally realized his absence.

"Oh," Loki chuckled. "He's been hanging out with a girl he met. Funny thing is he just met her downtown this morning and he's already completely smitten."

"Good for him," Jule said. "It's about time that man found a girl. I hope things work out for him."

"Indeed."

"When will we meet her?"

"I've instructed Bradley to keep any new friends or love interests away from the group, for now. We are in dangerous times and must take every precaution necessary to keep ourselves hidden and safe until the danger has passed."

"You think the Order is going to find us?" William asked.

"As long as we are smart about our actions and movements, I don't think so. I have people out there, who will remain unnamed, keeping a lookout for any suspicious activity from the Order here. So far, they have seen nothing worth mentioning. Let's hope it stays that way. Maybe we'll get lucky and they won't connect Jeff to us out here. Regardless, keep your wits about you and stay alert."

"Will do," William said with a nod of his head.

"So you two need to be careful with your little escapades tonight," Loki warned. "Make sure you're not being followed. If you feel any sort of hesitation whatsoever, Jule should not attempt the transformation. The Order will only target you if they see you expose your True Self. As long as they think you are still a human, you're safer."

"Noted."

"Jule, if tonight doesn't work I want you here again tomorrow. We will try every day to activate your gene. However, as the moon begins to wane it will be more difficult."

Jule nodded, accepting his request. "Sama, err *Rose*, explained to me about werewolves' weakness to silver, and corrected me on my understanding of it."

"Yes," Loki said as he returned to his seat and settled down. "Silver only inhibits your ability to rapidly heal and regenerate, it can't kill you on its own."

"Okay, well since I was taught wrong about that – thanks Hollywood – can you tell me about the others? I've seen Demonik outside in the sun but you say he is a vampire? How does that work?"

"Ah yes. Well, you see, like the silver's effects being exaggerated for werewolves, the sun's effects are also exaggerated when it comes to vampires. Vampires can be in sunlight, they are just more sensitive to it. They burn more easily, and if exposed to prolonged direct sunlight, they will eventually burn to death. The sun's brightness is too intense for their eyes, so that is why you will see Demonik wear his sunglasses all of the time. You may also notice that he usually wears long-sleeved shirts and pants, exposing as little of his skin as possible during the day."

"Oh, yeah!" Jule suddenly realized. It seemed so obvious to her now. "Are there any others?"

"Yes, but we don't have the time to get into that right now. The sun is going to set soon and you two better get going," Loki instructed as he ushered William and Jule to the front door.

They walked to William's red pickup truck and he politely opened the passenger door for her. She climbed in, strapping on her seat belt, and sat nervously. She didn't understand why she was feeling so anxious; she had spent plenty of time alone with William before, but something about this time felt different. William climbed in and as soon as he started the truck, loud metal music began blasting through the speakers, giving Jule a jump.

"Sorry." He turned the volume down to a reasonable level.

"It's okay," Jule chuckled. "I wasn't expecting that. You can turn it back up if you want."

William smiled with his gentle blue eyes, giving the slightest little wink. Jule's stomach fluttered and her cheeks flushed. She grinned and shyly turned her head away to gaze out the window.

"Are you hungry?" he asked. "Do you want to get something to eat before we head out there?"

"No, I'm okay. Wait – what do you mean by 'head out there'? Where are we going?" she questioned.

"To my house."

"Your house? Why? That doesn't seem like a good idea considering the danger Loki has been talking about. You want to try a transformation here in town?"

"Yes, I do have a house here in town, for convenience, but that's not where I'm taking you. We're going to my family's ranch. It's called Blood Moon Ranch and it's about forty miles outside of town bordering the National Forest. It's secluded and safe. We'll have all the privacy we need." He winked.

William turned the truck around and began driving up the road to their destination.

"I didn't know your family had a ranch."

"Not many do. It's my sanctuary so I am very particular about whom I bring there. Loki is the only one in the group that knows where it is."

They drove for miles with only the low-volume metal music playing and the hum of the engine, neither of them speaking a word.

They reached the county line twenty miles outside of town before William finally spoke.

"I've always wanted to take you to my ranch."

Jule, unable to think of something to say, remained silent.

"I always thought about you. I always wondered where you were and what you were doing, if you were okay," he confessed quietly. "You know, when you left."

"Really?" Jule was surprised by his confession and her heart began to flutter. "I thought about you too," she admitted shyly. "There were so many things that reminded me of you, I actually don't think I went a single day without thinking about you." She blushed and dropped her gaze nervously to the floor.

William reached his hand over to hers and held it tightly. Jule looked up and met his gaze and his kind blue eyes instantly made her heart melt. William turned his eyes back to the road, his smile never fading. Jule, still gleefully glowing herself, turned her gaze out the window towards the setting sun. She couldn't believe what was happening and began doubting it, doubting herself, her insecurities taking control of her thoughts. A wave of emotions flooded her mind with the positives and negatives.

Does he feel the same way about me as I do him? No, he's just being supportive. Does he like me too? Has he liked me this whole time? No, he just knows that I'm feeling anxious and he's being a good friend. William is a really sweet guy, after all.

Regardless of why he was holding her hand, Jule was thoroughly enjoying it and not about to let go.

Jule's heart sank a little as William released his grasp to adjust the rear-view mirror and make a hard right turn off the highway onto a dirt road. The sunlight was quickly fading and darkness started to take over, prompting William to turn on his headlights. Jule noticed he was frequently checking the rear-view mirror for something behind them.

"What's wrong?" Jule asked as she sat up to look out the back window. She saw nothing in the darkness except the red hue of the truck's taillights glowing off the dust trail behind them. She sat back down in her seat.

"I thought I saw a car behind us," he said. "No one else lives out this way. My ranch borders national forest and there's no camping sites out here so there shouldn't be anyone else on this road at night. If there is, we are probably being followed."

Jule began anxiously checking the mirrors, straining her eyes to see through the dust into the dark. William's obvious unease made Jule nervous. If he was worried, she should definitely be worried, too.

"What do we do if we are being followed?"

"I don't know, but you stay in the truck."

Jule nodded before turning her head around again to look out the back window. They continued down the road, climbing and bending with the hilly terrain.

"I don't see anything," Jule said as she sat back in her seat. "It's been a while. Do you still think we're being followed?"

"No, I guess not," he said with a sigh of relief. Jule noticed William's posture become more relaxed, which in turn made her feel a bit more at ease.. William reached over and found Jule's hand once again and she smiled as she tightly held his hand in her lap. His grasp was rough and worn – a working man's hands, but also had a soft and gentle feel to them. They drove in pleasant silence enjoying their small embrace.

After a long day of uncertainty, Jule knew one thing for sure: this was more than just a crush; she was in love with William.

CHAPTER 8

The high-beams of the truck illuminated an enormous iron arch over the road. At the top was a large red rusted moon with the words: "BLOOD MOON RANCH" painted on a wooden sign next to it.

"We're here," William announced.

Jule let go of his hand and adjusted herself in her seat, positioning herself to better see out the windshield. Though, in the darkness she could hardly make out any detail of her surroundings. The driveway was long and passed under a grove of sycamore trees on either side. They finally came upon a large two story log cabin, a lone ancient-looking elm tree with enormous branches outstretched in front of it.

"Welcome to my humble abode." William said with pride as he parked the truck. "Come on in."

Jule got out of the truck and followed William to the cabin. To call it a cabin was almost an insult; the structure was more like a log mansion than anything. Jule had never seen anything like it. Above the door was a hand-carved depiction of wolves howling at a moon. Going down either side of the door were carvings of the moon phases beginning with a full moon and ending with a new moon. She admired the intricate beauty.

Above her, high in the elm tree, a chorus of loud cawing ravens chanted in unison.

"Hey guys," William greeted the ruckus of corvids with a wave of his hand.

Jule looked at him in awe.

"These are the resident ravens," he chuckled as he explained. "I like having them around. They greet me every time I come home – they act as an early warning system as well. I also hunt with them occasionally and share my kills. They come in handy."

"That's really cool," Jule said with envy, always wanting a pet raven of her own.

"That one up there is King," he said, pointing to the very tip of the elm tree where a huge, regal raven sat looking down on them, his throat feathers fluffed out like a black mane as he cawed. "They mate for life and his mate died a few years ago. He's been alone ever since, but he kind of looks after the others. He's like their leader, or their *king*. Sometimes they even leave me little trinkets and stuff on my back porch. I think it's cute."

William opened the door and turned on the lights, illuminating a magnificent great room.

"Wow!" Jule gasped as she took in her surroundings. An enormous mounted elk head decorated the top of a floor-to-ceiling stone fireplace, the tips of the antlers nearly touching the ceiling. An elk antler chandelier hung in the center of the room. A spiral staircase with steel rails swirled to the second floor on the right. In the center of the room was a nine-foot grizzly bear rug, the vicious mouth agape bearing all of the beast's ferocious teeth and a stiff, curly pink tongue.

"This house has been in my family for many generations." William made his way across the room and turned on a small lamp made of deer antlers and a leather skin shade on a table next to a suede recliner. "Now it's mine."

"You don't have any other family here?" Jule felt ashamed that she never really knew anything about William's family life. She didn't know if he had any brothers or sisters or if he was an only child. She didn't even know if his parents were alive.

"No. My brother died in a car wreck about ten years ago. A drunk driver on the wrong side of the road hit him head-on. He was killed instantly. My parents are away for a few years. I can't really tell you much about that," he admitted and apologetically looked at Jule. "The rest of my family are fairly spread out back East, my cousins, aunts, uncles. So, it's just me here."

"Oh," Jule said quietly. "I'm sorry about your brother. That's awful."

"It happened a long time ago." William shrugged. "It's okay."

"So, how are we going to do this?" Jule asked nervously. She began fidgeting with her hands dangling down in front of her again.

"Well, the best place to do this would be outside, but we don't have to try the transformation right away. I can tell you're nervous about it. We can just hang out first until you're ready," he assured her.

"No, it's okay. I want to get this over with."

"Alright, if you're sure."

Jule sternly nodded with as much confidence as she could muster and took a deep breath.

"A fierce one, aren't you?" he joked.

Jule followed him to a glass double-door that opened to a wooden overhanging porch. Outside, choruses of crickets chirped loudly and the luminous full moon washed all but the brightest stars and planets away in the cloudless night sky. They went down a staircase to the side of the elevated porch into a large, open grass field. William came to a stop at a wide dirt clearing in the middle of the field where a fire pit had been dug and encircled with rocks and a pile of firewood stacked conveniently nearby. He knelt down next to the pit and removed some crumpled paper from his pocket, tossing it into the center. He then stood up and collected some dry grass from beyond the reaches of the fire pit and placed it onto the paper, topping it off with a few small branches. Jule watched as he removed a lighter from his pocket, striking it aflame and bringing his heap of wooden offerings to a humble fiery life. He blew at the base of the flame to give it extra oomph and the fire quickly took off, eagerly eating away at the fuel he offered it. Jule grabbed a log from the stack and placed it on the fire.

"Now what do we do?"

"Well, this is kind of awkward," William said. "But I have to undress in order to show you."

Jule blushed at the thought of seeing William naked. She can't say she hasn't fantasized about it and for her fantasy to come true made her anxious and giddy. She involuntarily let out a giggle.

"Ha," William said sarcastically. "Now, knowing that, do you want me to continue? I don't want to do anything that would make you feel uncomfortable."

"No, it's fine," Jule said. "I'm certainly not complaining." She couldn't help herself and giggled again.

Even through the orange glow of the fire, Jule could see William's cheeks flush bright red.

"Okay, here we go."

He kicked off his shoes to the perimeter of the circle, removed and tossed his socks to accompany his shoes, and clumsily stumbled around as he tried to remove his pants. Jule couldn't help but laugh at his struggle. He shot her a quick glance and then smirked as he finished removing his pants and threw them at Jule, smacking her in the face, sending them both into a hysterical yet nervous laughter. He removed his shirt and tossed it onto the heap of clothes. Jule stared at his lightly-haired chest, her heart rate quickening. William wasn't the type of guy who would strut around shirtless. Even seeing him relaxing at home Jule noticed that he seemed more comfortable in a shirt than without, often immediately putting one on if she were to arrive at his house unexpectedly.

She sensed a feeling of vulnerability from William, being so exposed in front of her for the first time. He stopped when he reached his boxers and looked up at her searching her eyes for approval. Jule smiled reassuringly at him and he blushed.

The light of the fire danced on William's uncovered torso, his abdominal muscles and pectorals glimmering seductively. Jule never realized how muscular he really was. Her blood began to turn hot, her cheeks flushing up again, her heart racing and pounding in her chest. She tried to be respectful and not stare at him, but her eyes wouldn't look away. Her unspoken love and attraction to him prevented her from turning her attention anywhere else. He was magnificent and Jule wanted to hold him, to feel his bare skin against hers. She wanted to be so close to him that their bodies would meld into one. Her intense feelings startled her a bit; she had never felt this way about anyone before and she wasn't sure if he felt the same. If he didn't, her heart would surely be crushed. William was everything Jule had ever wanted. To her, he was absolutely perfect and rejection from him would truly be devastating.

William stood awkwardly, shifting his feet beneath him as his eyes lowered to the ground. Jule impulsively stood up and rushed to wrap her arms around him, burying her face in his warm chest, feeling his beating heart against her cheek and the tickle of his chest hairs on her nose. Her sudden embrace made William momentarily tense up. He relaxed and tightly hugged Jule in his arms, resting his cheek on the top of her head.

He pulled back and caressed Jule's face in his hands as she looked up at him, then he leaned in and their lips met in a gentle kiss.

William's kiss sent a jolt of electricity throughout Jule's entire body, from her fingertips all the way down to her toes. She was ecstatic. His was the sweetest, most sincere and loving kiss Jule had ever experienced in her life. His energy seemed to flow through her, filling her whole body with a warm, fuzzy sensation.

He pulled his lips away from hers just enough to whisper to her. "There was this indescribable feeling that came over me when I first laid eyes on you, and now I know, it was love at first sight."

Jule felt like she was going to melt in his arms.

"I love you, too," she whispered, declaring her feelings for him aloud for the first time.

She grasped him tightly, never wanting to let go. His confession of love sent a whirlwind of emotions through her. She wanted to cry from happiness and shout her love for him to the world. Jule couldn't believe this was truly happening. Had she found her soulmate? Was William really meant for her all along? They sealed their lips together sharing the most passionate, intimate kiss under the light of the full moon. William gently laid Jule on the ground, their lips never parting, and rested his body on top of hers. She wrapped her arms tightly around his torso enveloping her body around his. The tangled lovers kissed and cuddled in front of the fire finally embracing their discovered mutual love for each other.

"I always hoped it would be you," she whispered softly into his ear.

He pulled back away from her to look her in the eye. "I never thought I would have a chance with you. I never thought I was good enough. The moment I first met you all those years ago my soul knew you were the one for me. I knew we had to be together, but my heart also knew that you were young —too young for that kind of commitment. I knew I had to let you run wild and free and hope that someday I could have you again. Now, you've managed to run right back into my arms, and here we are."

He paused for a moment.

"Jule, you and I are meant for each other. You are my soul mate."

"Why didn't you tell me how you felt before?"

William looked down nervously at the ground and fidgeted at the dirt with his finger. "I don't know. I didn't think you would be interested in me and I really cherished our friendship so I didn't want take the chance of ruining it."

Jule laughed. "That's ridiculous."

"Well, why didn't *you* say anything before?" he challenged.

"For the same reason I guess. I never thought you would like me like that," she said quietly. "You deserve some gorgeous super model, not me." She gestured with her hand to herself. "Hell, I don't even wear makeup and I don't think I'm very pretty."

William chuckled. "Now *that's* ridiculous. That's why I love you; you're not like any other woman that I've met before, and you're absolutely beautiful without makeup. You don't need it. You have true natural beauty."

Jule blushed again as he rolled over with her, placing her body on top of his and she rested her head on his shoulder. William wrapped his arm around her as they gazed into the fading flames of the dying fire, their cheeks pressed together.

"I almost forgot why we even came out here," he said. "Do you still want me to show you? I mean, I'm enjoying just being nearly naked around you, but..." he chuckled.

"Oh yeah," Jule replied. "Let's finish what we came out here for. I'll put another log on the fire."

Jule stood up and fed the fire a piece of juniper. It crackled with joy and a large ember popped out in response. Jule quickly stomped on it to extinguish the ember and sat back down in the dirt across from William.

He took a deep breath and then proceeded to remove his boxers and tossed them to the side, standing in front of Jule completely exposed. Instinctively he covered his groin with his hands, but he wasn't fast enough for Jule's quick eyes. She couldn't help but get a sneak peek at what he had to offer. She was impressed, and smiled coyly. William continued with his task and got down on his hands and knees in the soft dirt closing his eyes.

"Now, what I'm doing is envisioning my transformation," he explained. "I try to remember every painful detail of my body shifting as it changes. I imagine myself in my final wolf form. You will feel pain every time, each change hurts but it gets easier the more you do it."

As he spoke Jule noticed his teeth began lengthening and sharpening, his nails began growing into sharp ferocious claws, and hair began sprouting from every pore on his body.

Jule nodded as she watched his transformation in awe. He writhed on the ground and moaned quietly in pain, his moans becoming more animal-like than human as the seconds passed. She noticed that his change was quick, much quicker than her first transformation it seemed. He let out one longer growl that faded into a low howl. Where William was just standing naked and vulnerable, now stood a mighty black wolf with haunting blue eyes staring intently at Jule.

Jule gasped at his magnificence. He lightly wagged his tail and approached her. His size was incredible, much larger than the wolf she met at Sama's cabin. They stood eye-to-eye.

She reached out her hand and gently pet the fur on his head down his neck and to his back. His fur was thick and wiry but had an underlying softness to it. He closed his eyes and leaned against her, almost knocking her over with his weight.

"Wow," Jule said. "I hardly recognize you."

The wolf let out a small, broken growl as if he was trying to laugh with her but his new vocal chords weren't capable of laughter. He then lifted his head, pointing his nose towards his back as if to signal Jule to get on.

"You want me to climb on?" she asked the wolf skeptically.

He nodded and lowered his stance, dropping his shoulders down to give Jule easier access to his back.

"Alright," Jule said as she hesitantly climbed on and tightly gripped the fur on his neck with both hands, leaning forward. William took off with a mighty leap, bounding clear over the fire and rushing out into the open field. Jule had experience riding horses before, but the wolf's gait contained far more power and agility than that of a horse. She struggled to hang on during the exhilarating ride as William leapt and bounded with absolute grace, effortlessly twisting this way and that in a serpentine motion, the grass whipping Jule in the face as they raced by.

Suddenly William came to a halt, nearly throwing Jule over his head. She could feel his muscles quivering beneath her legs.

"What's wrong?" Jule asked as she followed the wolf's gaze.

He glared ahead towards the tree line, focusing his eyes to see beyond the trees. She wished now that she had her acute wolf eyes to see with, for her human eyes were weak and pathetic and couldn't see very far at all. The wolf lowered his stance once again and Jule took the silent instruction to dismount. He looked her in the eye, pawed at the ground and snorted. Jule interpreted his message as a "stay here", so she knelt quietly in the grass as the wolf tore off to investigate, quickly disappearing into the pine woods across the field with astounding speed. Jule was breathing hard from excitement and could barely hear anything over her own pulse pounding in her head. She focused on slowing her breath and her heart, straining to hear anything above the crickets. Her pathetic human ears failed her.

There was nothing.

A few moments later the wolf loped back up to her and gave the signal to mount again. They quickly returned to the fire. Jule dismounted once again and William trotted over across from her to transform back into his human form.

"What was it?" Jule asked as he finished his transformation and stood before her naked once again.

He gathered up his clothes and quickly redressed.

"I thought I smelled something strange in the air, something foreign, so I went to go check it out. I lost the scent in the trees though and couldn't pick it back up. I think we're fine, no need to worry." He turned to her. "Are you ready for your turn now?"

Jule nodded. "I'm ready."

"Well, you have to get undressed, too," he said. "The clothes are too constraining and you'll shred them when you change. I'll give you some privacy."

William politely turned his back to her as she hesitantly removed her clothes and piled them neatly out of the way. She got down on her hands and knees in the dirt as William did and took a deep breath.

"Remember, you really have to *envision* yourself changing. Will it to happen," he reminded her without turning around. "Use the experience you had with Rose to guide you."

Jule focused on the wolf she was earlier that day. She focused on the crunching noises her bones made, the twisting and contorting pain of her muscles and tendons as they shifted in her body. She began to feel a familiar pain in the pit of her stomach and an itching sensation all over her skin. The pain intensified and she let out a miserable moan.

"Don't fight it, Jule," William coaxed.

"I… can't… do… it…" Jule stammered. "It's too painful. I'm trying!"

She was showing no signs of an actual physical change no matter how hard she concentrated and willed it. After several minutes of failing her transformation, Jule collapsed exhausted to the ground, her muscles trembling and aching.

"I can't do it," she whimpered, feeling defeated with tears dancing in her eyes.

"It's okay," William said as he gently wrapped Jule up in his jacket. "Let's get you dressed."

He helped Jule back into her clothes, stamping out the fire as she finished. Too weak to walk herself, he carried her cradled in his arms back to the cabin, placing her gently on the couch inside the living room under the elk antler chandelier.

"Do you want something to drink?" he offered.

"Some water would be nice," Jule replied, curling up in a ball on the couch.

She felt foolish and ashamed. Toxic thoughts of failure spun wildly in her mind. Jule began doubting whether she really was a werewolf or if it was all some cruel trick. No matter how much she tried or how much she focused with all her might, she couldn't transform into a wolf. She was still just a human when she desperately wanted to be more. Tears of frustration rolled down her cheeks. All she wanted was to truly belong somewhere and now she felt like it was all just a tease, merely a taste of inclusion and belonging.

William returned from the kitchen down the hallway and placed a glass of ice water on the coffee table in front of her.

"Are you okay?" he asked as he sat down beside her, the remnants of tears lingering on her cheeks.

"I'm fine," she lied as she quickly wiped her eyes.

"Come on, what's wrong?" he pressed.

Jule looked up into his soft eyes, another tear involuntarily welling up. William wiped it away as it fell down her cheek with a gentle stroke of his thumb, then held her face gently in his warm hand and leaned forward to kiss her pouting lips.

"I'm just really upset that I couldn't do it," she admitted quietly as their lips parted. "I mean, are you sure I'm one of you?"

Jule looked him hard in his eyes desperately seeking an answer. He wrapped his arms tightly around her and Jule snuggled her face into his chest.

"I know you are, Jule," he assured her.

"How though?" she asked. "I couldn't change. Nothing happened."

"Honestly," he said, "I can smell it in your blood."

Jule looked up at William puzzled.

"You can smell my blood?" she asked.

"Yes and you don't have to be bleeding for me to smell it. I can smell your blood as easily as I can smell your sweat or your deodorant. You have lycan blood. You are one of us and you do belong here. You belong with me."

Jule felt comforted by his words and snuggled up next to him. William tightened his arms around her and held her close. She wanted, more than anything, to belong with him. William pulled down the blanket draped on the back of the couch and covered them both with it. Jule, still exhausted from exerting so much effort in vain, fell asleep with ease to the rhythm of William's heartbeat.

CHAPTER 9

The early morning sun peered through the window onto the lovers tightly woven together in a huddled mess on the couch. A beam of light pierced through Jule's closed eyelids and stirred her awake. She took a long stretch reaching her arms out, accidentally smacking William in the face.

"Ow!" he exclaimed as he woke.

"Oh, I'm sorry!" Jule laughed, completely embarrassed.

William chuckled and shook his head at her.

"How about some coffee?" he asked as he stood up and stretched.

His shirt rose slightly as he stretched his arms far above his head. Jule caught a glimpse of his exposed torso, his muscles tightening with his reach. Her cheeks flushed and her stomach fluttered with lust.

William caught Jule's stare and smirked with a wink, then removed his shirt completely.

"Better view?" he teased with sudden confidence.

Jule blushed and buried her face in the blanket shyly. William leapt onto the couch and quickly pulled the blanket out of her grasp. They gleamed at each other as they held their gaze, his blue eyes peering down into hers with love and laughter. The two once again entangled themselves in a lover's mess and passionately kissed. William slipped his hand up the back of her shirt caressing her arched back, pulling her pelvis into his. He leaned in to whisper in her ear, his hot breath sending shivers of ecstasy through her body.

"I love you, Jule," he said, his lips tickling her ear as he spoke.

"I love you," she whispered. "Now, how about some coffee?" she asked as she slowly pulled away.

Never feeling a love for someone this intense before made Jule nervous. She was uncertain in how to handle her feelings and was beginning to feel overwhelmed, but at the same time she was completely thrilled with her newfound love. Was she finally ready to let down her guard and let someone into her life? She had been alone for so long now, shunning every advance thrown at her for the sake of her own personal peace. Too many painful, failed and toxic relationships made her reluctant to the idea, but William was someone she had wanted for a very long time. He was different.

"Of course." William kissed her cheek as he stood up and headed to the kitchen.

Jule sat on the couch and bundled herself up in the blanket, still trying to fully grasp all that was happening. William was a shape-shifting creature who was in love with her. Supposedly she, too, was a shape-shifting creature. All of this seemed so unbelievable to Jule, as if she was living in a dream and would wake up to being back in her boring life again at any moment. She wished desperately that if this was a dream, she would never wake up from it.

"We will head over to Loki's when you're ready," William announced as he returned with hot, fresh coffee.

"Thank you," she said as she took a sip. "I completely forgot about going to Loki's today."

"Yeah, he wants to see you and he's going to want to know how your attempt went last night."

"Pfft, I failed miserably," Jule said with a frown.

"Hey, that's fine. No one expects you to be able to transform right away. You weren't born into this lifestyle like I was. You weren't taught about who you are since you were a child, as I was. You're starting out late in the game, which is always more difficult, but I'll be here to help you." His voice quivered with worry and concern as he finished his sentence and dropped his gaze to his hands clasping his olive green coffee mug. Something about his tone made Jule worry.

"What is it?" Jule pressed him to explain his grim expression.

"What Loki may have to subject you to…" he trailed off.

"What?" Jule pressed again, needing to know.

"He may have to basically torture you. I don't know if I can stand to witness that. Just the thought of someone hurting you makes my blood boil," he quietly admitted with sadness in his eyes.

Jule's heart jumped at the word "torture".

"Well, he did say he would start out with easier stuff, right? Maybe it won't take much to trigger my True Self." She attempted to sound optimistic, but her voice shook with fear instead. William hugged her tight and kissed her gently on the forehead. They finished their coffees in silence, William's arm still wrapped around Jule, holding her close. Jule's thoughts erratically spun around in her head, chaotically jumping all over the place as she imagined various torture scenarios.

William took the last sip of his coffee and firmly set it on the table in front of them.

"Well," he said. "Ready to go?"

"Sure I guess." Jule replied, snapping back to reality.

They gathered their things and headed out the door. The ravens cawed at the sight of William, King standing on the tailgate of his truck. Jule noticed that their cries seemed to be more alarming than when they first arrived, with King's wings spread wide and jumping back and forth on the tailgate before flying off to the top of the tree. William paused at his truck and looked around, sniffing the air with suspicion.

"What's wrong?" Jule asked, also glancing around anxiously but unsure of what she was looking for.

"That same smell from last night that I lost in the woods, I caught a faint sniff of it again. Whatever it is, it's still around and the neighborhood watch doesn't approve."

"Should we be concerned?"

"No." William said firmly. "Just get in the truck and let's leave."

Jule promptly followed his demand. They took off out of the driveway kicking up dust as William spun the tires. He appeared to be trying to outrun whatever he sensed nearby as quickly as possible. Jule anxiously held onto the door handle and tightened her seat belt. Once they reached the paved road William slowed the vehicle down to a more legal limit.

"Do you think we were followed last night?" Jule finally broke the uneasy silence.

"I don't know, honestly. The scent didn't smell human. It was something I've never smelled before; I don't recognize it. That's what makes me worried – not knowing *what* it is."

He reached over and clasped Jule's hand tightly in his, looking at her with worry in his soft, handsome blue eyes. Jule had never seen him like this before. William was always so confident and sure of himself during times of potential threat. She recalled several times when she witnessed him in a bar fight, completely capable of holding his own. Now, though, he seemed more vulnerable than when he stood naked before Jule the previous night. She gave his hand a light squeeze and gently stroked the top of it with her thumb. They both silently turned their gaze out the windshield, still vigilantly checking the mirrors for someone tailing them, their hands never parting.

By the time they reached Loki's house their nerves had calmed. Jule ignored the unknown danger and found herself distracted in blissful love.

Loki was standing outside waiting for their arrival. He waved them down as they got out of William's truck.

"Good morning guys!" he greeted.

"Morning!" Jule and William said in unison, walking hand-in-hand. Loki noticed a new glow about them.

"So, by the looks of it, I can assume that last night was a success?"

William and Jule looked at each other, clear disappointment written all over their faces.

"Well, not exactly," Jule explained. "I wasn't able to transform. William talked me through the whole thing and I really tried, but no matter what I did I just couldn't make the change."

She frowned as the feeling of defeat came over her once again. William squeezed her hand and lovingly smiled, making a small but genuine attempt to cheer her up.

"Oh," Loki said softly, sharing in their disappointment. "The next part isn't going to be easy, Jule, and I want you to know that I absolutely take no pleasure in what may have to happen. I'm doing this to help you become what you really are. That's what you want, isn't it?"

Jule nodded her head. "Yes... more than anything."

"Come inside and we'll talk," Loki instructed as he invited them in.

William and Jule, still hand-in-hand, followed Loki into the house.

"So I have to ask, what's up with that?" Loki asked as he gestured to the couple's grasp.

William and Jule exchanged glances with each other and Jule blushed.

"I don't know," William began, "I guess we're together now?"

He looked at Jule for confirmation. Jule nodded in agreement and smiled, letting go of his hand and wrapping her arm around his waist with pride.

"Okay then." Loki grinned, approving of the union. "I was wondering when that was going to happen," he chuckled and took a seat in his lounge chair.

William and Jule sat together on the couch across from him.

"We must discuss what we are going to do with you now," Loki explained. "What the next step is."

Jule released William's hand and sat forward, waiting for Loki to continue.

"Like I said before, we'll start light, but the less you respond the more intense the method will have to be."

William began gently stroking Jule's back with the tips of his fingers, her muscles tensing as Loki went on.

"I am going to be completely honest with you; I may have to hurt you," he said with regret.

Jule unintentionally gave a slight jump.

"How?" she asked.

"Worst case scenario, you may have some broken bones, but Rayme will be on-hand at all times to tend to your medical needs. We'll go at your pace. If you can't handle it, tell me to stop, but we will have to push you."

"And you'll stop?" she asked, concerned.

Loki ignored her question and continued.

"We will start today. The sooner we begin, the better. Time isn't exactly on our side."

Jule nodded reluctantly. What else could she do? She considered running for the door, getting into William's truck and driving away as far as she could, but her longing for that feeling of ultimate freedom as a wolf pulled at her. She mustered up what courage she could, preparing herself to endure whatever Loki had in mind for her. She yearned to be like them, to be different, to be more than human. She fantasized about running rampant through the woods side-by-side with her soul mate. To feel wild and free. To feel powerful. To feel *something*.

"I'm ready." Jule declared with shaken confidence.

"We have to wait for Rayme to arrive before we begin. He should be here any moment. Come downstairs with me and I will show you the first test."

Loki showed the way to a door near the back of the house, a door Jule had never gone through or even noticed before. She assumed it was a storage area or possibly where the water heater was located. Loki turned the knob of the creaky wooden door and revealed a brightly lit and very clean medical-looking facility down some metal grated stairs. Surgical tools lay displayed on shiny metal trays to the side of a steel table in the middle of the room illuminated by a large, bright lamp that hung above. Brown leather restraints hung dangling off of the sides of the table, the buckles lying on the floor. Something glistening drew Jule's attention to a metal drain located in the center of the floor. *This is a dangerous room,* she thought bleakly to herself. Slowly and with hesitation, she followed Loki down the stairs. Taking the last step, Jule's eyes followed the walls of the room spanning the length of the house, six bright fluorescent hood lamps in pairs hanging from the ceiling all the way down. He took a seat in a spinning chair by a desk off to the side of the room and gestured to Jule to sit down in a metal folding chair positioned a few feet away from him. William stood by the base of the stairs, arms crossed, his stance rigid and clearly uncomfortable as he leaned against the stone wall.

Jule sat across from Loki, nervous sweat perspiring from her forehead and armpits.

"I am going to ask you something and I want you to be completely honest about it. Your answer could be very important and useful in this process."

Jule nodded and waited for him to continue.

"What is your biggest fear?" Loki asked as he pressed his index fingers together against his lips and waited for her answer.

"Honestly," Jule stuttered, "drowning. I almost drowned in my grandpa's pool when I was really little. Ever since then, I've been terrified of water and the possibility of drowning."

"Well that is an easy one to work with," Loki said, leaning back in his chair.

"What do you mean?"

"I am going to water board you."

"You're going to what!?" Jule exclaimed.

"Water board you. You know, put a cloth over your face and pour water over it to imitate the sensation of drowning," he simply answered.

"Like I'm some sort of interrogation subject?"

"Due to the fact that drowning is your number one fear, water boarding will be the most likely thing to trigger your transformation, I believe. The instinctual 'fight or flight' reaction is an excellent way to trigger an ability and awaken the gene. It forces the body to react in such a way to protect itself from termination – or death – that it could give your ability the spark it needs to kick-start it." He snapped his fingers. "Your body will do everything it can, without you thinking about it or controlling it, to survive the drowning. In most cases, that will be enough to trigger the ability."

Jule suddenly jumped as a loud pounding came from the front door upstairs. Without a word, William turned around and trotted up to answer it.

"That would probably be Rayme, tell him we're down here and ready for him would you?" Loki shouted after him. "Now, Jule, let's get you ready. That's yours." He pointed to an odd wooden chair with metal arms resting against the wall, a bundle of rope coiled on the floor next to it. "Bring it over here, don't worry about the rope."

Loki wheeled the menacing torture table further down the room, the straps dangling and dragging along the floor, positioning it snug against the wall out of the way. Jule shivered as she reluctantly obeyed, pulling the chair away from the wall, positioning it as she was directed, and sat down placing her arms on the cold metal. She watched nervously as Loki picked up the rope and began binding her to the chair, fastening her wrists together in front of her with her hands folded in her lap, securing her arms to her sides with the rope firmly wrapped around the back of the chair to the front of her chest, making it difficult to breathe. Her ankles held apart individually fastened to the legs of the chair. Her heart began pounding wildly in her chest, her breathing becoming rapid, her chest getting tighter and tighter with each breath. Loki removed a red bandanna out of a drawer in the desk, rolled it up and tied it around Jule's face forcing the bandanna into her mouth between her teeth.

"This room is mostly soundproof. I'm fairly certain that no one will be able to hear you if you should scream," he explained as he tightened the bandanna. The corners of her mouth immediately started to hurt from the pressure. She bit down on the cloth in her mouth, grinding her teeth against it.

Loki flipped the chair over without warning. Jule's heart jumped as she landed hard on her back, her head hitting the concrete floor beneath her, dazing her for a moment.

"Hey man!" William exclaimed defensively as he rushed down the stairs. "Was that really necessary?"

"Anything I can do to scare her works best, William. If you can't handle this – if you're going to be more of a hindrance than a help, I am going to have to ask you to leave now," Loki firmly stated.

William started to say something but decided against it and respectfully held his tongue. He shook his head and leaned back hard against the wall, arms crossed firmly in front of him again.

"Just, try to be careful with her, please," he grumbled.

Rayme approached Jule tightly bound on the floor.

"Hello Jule," He smiled kindly down at her.

Jule grunted through the gag in response. Her wrists and ankles were beginning to ache from her struggling against the tight rope and her head was pounding from striking the floor. Loki pulled a large, clean, dark heavy cloth from another drawer in the desk and draped it over her face shielding her eyes and rendering her blind. She heard Loki's footsteps click across the concrete floor as he walked around her, a metal bucket clanging into the side of a sink and then being filled with water followed. Jule's heart raced, pounding heavily in her chest. Every moment that passed felt longer than the last as she waited in excruciating anticipation for the inevitable water and the terrifying feeling of drowning. Footsteps approached her along with the sloshing of water in a metal can.

"Here we go," Loki warned as he raised the bucket and tilted it over her face. Water poured heavily onto the cloth sending Jule into spasmodic jolts as she strained to free herself from the chair. Water made its way into her nostrils and she began choking, jerking her head from side to side, trying desperately to escape it. The torture felt like it would never end, that Loki wouldn't stop in time and she feared that she would actually drown. Water filled her mouth through the bandanna and she began choking it down, desperately gasping for air through the gag and inhaling more fluid instead.

Finally, after what felt like an eternity, the water suddenly stopped. Loki rested the bucket on the floor with a clang and pulled the cloth off her face. Leaving her lying uncomfortably bound to the chair on the floor, he pulled the bandanna down to her chin, allowing her to finally breathe. She greedily gasped in deep gulps of air, coughing and expelling water from her lungs. Loki turned the chair over on to its side, allowing her to vomit the water she swallowed down the drain and patted her hard on the back.

"There you go," he coaxed. "Get it out. Breathe. I'm going to flip you back over and do it again."

Jule panicked, she couldn't go through it again.

"No, no, no!" she cried in desperation, tears streaming down her face. Her arms and legs struggled to free themselves from the restraints to no avail.

Loki ignored her pleas, replaced her gag and fastened it tightly, turning the chair over onto its back once again. Jule raised her head in time to miss striking the concrete. She winced as he plopped the wet rag onto her face and proceeded to pour water over her once more. Jule jerked and twisted in vain. Her arms and legs struggled to get loose. She tried desperately to avoid the water getting into her nose and mouth again by raising her head, turning it this way and that, but failed. She began choking and coughing, her body trembling from exhaustion. She wanted him to stop but couldn't express her wishes. She was completely at his mercy. If he didn't stop in time, she would drown.

Once again, the water ceased and Loki removed the rag. The bright lights shone painfully in her face and she grimaced. Loki turned the chair over, removing her gag and loosening the ropes. She collapsed forward onto the cold wet floor, shivering and coughing, gasping for air. William rushed to her side quickly wrapping her tightly in a thick blanket, cradling her head in his lap and vigorously rubbing her back to warm her up.

"Well, that didn't work," Rayme stated. "Let me take a look at you."

He knelt down beside Jule, lifting her head up and shining a pen light into her eyes, waving it back and forth.

"How do you feel?" he asked.

"Terrible, cold, and tired," she replied as she trembled in William's arms. "That was the worst thing I have ever experienced in my life." Her voice shook as she spoke. Her heart slowed and her tired limbs lay draped weakly on the floor.

"Can you breathe alright now?" Rayme asked.

Jule nodded.

"How's your head?" Rayme inspected the back of her skull.

"It hurts like fucking hell."

"I think she just needs to rest," William said protectively.

"I agree," Loki said. "Let's get her upstairs."

Loki knelt down beside Jule and asked her, "Can you walk?"

"I don't know. I'm still dizzy and my legs are really shaky. I can try." She attempted to find her feet.

Loki and William held either of her arms, helping her to stand. Her legs trembled and suddenly gave beneath her. William swiftly scooped her up into his arms before she hit the ground and held her close to his chest.

"I'll just carry her," he told Loki.

Loki nodded without argument and they headed back upstairs to the main part of the house. William gently laid Jule down on the couch and sat on the floor next to her, gently petting her hair and kissing her forehead as her body shook and shivered.

"So you two, huh?" Rayme asked as he saw the affection exchanged between them.

"Yeah," William chuckled and turned back to Jule.

"Well that's cute," Rayme stated with a grin. He adjusted his square glasses on the bridge of his nose with a long, slender index finger.

"I'm sorry Jule," Loki said as he offered her a fresh cup of hot coffee.

"It's okay." She sat up and gladly accepted Loki's offering, sipping the hot coffee, warming her hands on the warm mug. The hot, bitter liquid worked its magic in her body, warming her with each gulp. *It could use a little more creamer and a pinch more sugar*, she thought to herself.

Loki walked over to a hand carved wooden box about 6 inches wide and 4 inches tall that rested on the table behind the couch. With a grin on his face he lifted the lid and removed a joint, lighting it as he sat down in his chair. He took a deep inhale, slowly breathing the smoke out with a big sigh.

"Here, you look like you could use this." Loki smiled, offering Jule the joint.

"That's what I was going to suggest, actually," declared Rayme as he sat down.

"Gladly," she said and took a big puff of the aromatic joint. With a smooth exhale of the smoke her anxiety almost instantly began melting away. She sat back in the couch, taking another long drag, and passed it to William. The four of them continued puffing and passing the joint, relaxing in their seats as they laughed and told jokes. Loki slipped another joint out from the back of his ear and lit it up. The room quickly filled with more thick smoke and the small giggling group found temporary relief from the terrifying, stressful event that just took place.

"So, what do I have to endure next?" Jule finally asked Loki, now comfortable enough to talk about it.

"Well, next we move on to more pain-oriented methods rather than fear-oriented. The next step is to shock you."

Before Jule could react, the front door opened and Bradley walked in.

"Hey guys," he greeted the group.

"Hey!" they all responded in unison.

"Where have you been?" Jule asked.

Bradley walked into the living room and snatched what was left of the joint out of Loki's hand, taking a greedy couple of puffs before snuffing it out in the ashtray on the table.

"I spent the night at a, uh, friend's house," Bradley said after a coughing fit.

"So, who's this new 'friend'?" William teased.

Bradley noticed the closeness of William and Jule with a puzzled expression, then nodded in approval.

"Oh, she's just some girl I met downtown yesterday," he said nonchalantly.

"What's her name?" William pressed on, looking for more than vague details.

"Her name is Marie," Bradley answered. "She's not from here. Apparently she has some family here and she's visiting them for a few weeks, so unfortunately I think whatever this is will be short-lived."

"That's too bad," said Jule.

"Hey, enjoy the moment, right?" Bradley cheered.

"When do we get to meet her?" asked Rayme, who was not present for Loki's warning the previous day.

"You won't," Loki said sternly, not giving his brother the chance to respond. "Due to the delicacy of our current situation I have instructed Bradley to not introduce his new 'friend' to anyone in the group and to certainly not bring her to our house. We can't be too careful right now, with rumor of the Order sulking about."

"Did you hear something from your anonymous spies?" Rayme asked.

"Yes, actually. Two agents have been spotted at a truck stop on the highway about sixty miles from here. Two large men from what I've been told. They were seen driving a brown Chevy SUV but my *spies*, as you say, lost track of them outside of town. These agents are impressively cunning if they managed to lose them."

Rayme and William nodded in agreement to the extra precautions that seemed necessary.

"I'm sorry Bradley, but that's just the way it has to be, at least for now."

"I know," he said. "It's fine. We can always hang out at the bar."

Rayme stood up and approached Jule on the couch, kneeling down in front of her.

"Are you feeling better?" he asked as he examined her closely looking for signs of trauma.

"Yeah, I'm okay now, much better. I'm really not looking forward to the next step though. Why does this have to be so intense?"

"We need to take advantage of the power of the full moon, so I apologize but I have to subject you to some harsh treatments. We will take a break as the moon wanes, but until then we have to try," Loki explained.

Jule nodded. She cogitated over the events to come and wondered if she would ever succeed in becoming her True Self.

CHAPTER 10

Exhausted from the morning's events, Jule drove in a trance back to Lillith's house, seeking some much needed peace and quiet. She parked her car in the driveway and greeted the happy, barking dogs as she walked up to the guest house. She placed her phone on the nightstand and plopped heavily face-down on the bed, not bothering to kick off her boots before curling up into a ball and closing her eyes.

Her phone rang noisily startling her from her deep slumber.

CALL FROM LOKI

"Hello?" Jule tiredly answered. She looked out the window to get a sense of what time it was. Night had fallen. *I must have been asleep for a few hours,* she thought to herself.

"Jule, it's Loki. Listen, I need you to come down to the bar right away. Something has come up."

"Okay, yeah sure," she replied, more alert. "I'll be there."

"Good." Loki hung up.

Jule briskly changed her dirty clothes and brushed her hair, rushing out the door. Lillith stepped outside just as Jule was getting into her vehicle.

"Hey where are you going?" Lillith called out to her.

"I have to run down to the bar. Loki needs me."

Jule didn't give Lillith any time for more questions and quickly sped off to the L&B Bar which sat on the corner of the main intersection downtown. It was a large two-story red brick building with white framed windows, the bar being at floor level and the office sat above it. Jule pulled her car around to the back of the bar near the alleyway and parked. As she walked toward the back door of the brick building she noticed Athan's vehicle as well as Catarina's maroon sedan parked out on the street. Jule opened the door and walked in, nearly colliding with Esadora.

"Woah hey!" Esadora exclaimed as Jule stepped to the side to avoid the collision.

"Hey you're here! What's going on?" Jule asked as she gave Esadora a quick hug.

"I don't know, Loki called everyone here for some major announcement. He even made Azul leave work. Come on, everyone else is upstairs in the office."

The bar was empty and quiet but Jule could faintly hear voices murmuring as she went further into the building. The two girls walked through maze of pool tables and bar stools to the staircase behind the bar and entered the office. Everyone seemed to be present, except for William, Loki, and Bradley. The hum of conversation buzzed in the air. Esadora and Jule made their way to a window that overlooked the damp downtown street below. Jule cracked it open and lit up a cigarette.

"Where did Loki go?" Jule asked.

"He went to try and track down Bradley. I guess has been hanging around a new female friend," Esadora answered with a shrug of her shoulders.

"Ha, yeah, so I've heard."

Jule quietly smoked her cigarette as she observed the room. Demonik, Viktor, Azul, and Catarina had invaded all of the possible space that a small love seat in the corner of the office had to offer. Catarina's long legs draped over Demonik's lap and her arm lazily hung around his neck as she sat upon him like a throne. She had a strong sexual presence and always looked like she was on the prowl for her next romantic victim. She wore a corset-style top that boosted her already full breasts quite dramatically and enhanced her thin hourglass figure. She wore knee-high black boots, a black miniskirt, and fishnet stockings that crept up her legs. Her full red lips stood out pouting from her pale flawless skin. She radiated with a lustful prowess. Catarina's confidence and beauty was immensely intimidating, making Jule feel quite inferior.

Azul, sitting between Demonik and Viktor, heavily puffed on a cigarette, clearly agitated, his eyes darting wildly around the room. Athan and Rayme stood opposite of Jule and Esadora deeply engaged in conversation, but the noise of the room drowned out their words, leaving Jule curious about their topic of discussion. Fidelia hovered nearby Catarina but her mind seemed to be wandering off in her own little world.

Jule finished her cigarette and flicked it out the window onto the damp street below. The downtown neon signs flashed and flickered brightly, illuminating the puddles of rain collected in the street. It was pretty quiet down there. Jule noticed there were far less people on the strip than usual for a Friday night.

Loki, followed closely by William, stormed through the door. His grand entrance immediately silenced the room. Everyone looked at him waiting for his announcement. William quietly closed the door behind him then leaned heavily against it with his arms crossed. Jule and William's eyes met and they exchanged affectionate smiles. Esadora noticed the exchange and gave Jule a light bump with her elbow, grinning and giving her a thumbs-up. Jule blushed and turned her attention back to Loki who looked very distraught.

"Well I can't find Bradley –" he began saying to the group, "—so we will have to continue without him and I will fill him in later, whenever I find him."

"What's this all about? You called me away from work. What's so important that I have to lose money by being here?" Azul angrily growled as he flicked his cigarette to the floor and stomped it out with his heavy steel-toe boot.

"I have received confirmation that the Order of Purity is here," Loki stated. He paused and scanned the room for a moment. His announcement restarted the buzz of conversation. William remained silent and stood firmly against the door, as if he was guarding it from an expected intruder.

"Quiet down please," Loki continued. "My anonymous source has felt the presence of the Order nearby. We aren't sure how many are here, or why they are here, or where they are. It could be a routine patrol taking reports on our area which we can easily avoid if we play it smart." Loki shot a threatening glare to the group occupying the love seat. "It could also be an agent who has been led here through the connections of Jeff's death. Either way, we need to be extra cautious."

"We should hunt this agent down!" Azul roared. "Why should we be hiding in fear from these pathetic religious humans?"

Catarina, Demonik, and Viktor shouted out in approval of Azul's defiance.

"No!" Loki shouted. "Now is not the time to go after them. We are safe, and if we continue being discrete, we will stay that way. As long as they don't find us, whoever it is will eventually move on. We cannot risk exposing ourselves."

A few of the others mumbled in agreement.

"Discrete is safe," said Athan, who quietly repeated his statement to himself.

Suddenly, a thud hit the door with such force that it knocked William stumbling forward. All eyes turned to him. Loki slowly stood up and approached as William returned to his guarding position, holding the door closed.

Everyone else backed up into the corner of the room as Loki ordered William to open the door. William hesitantly leaned his weight off of the door, keeping his hands firmly against it ensuring it wouldn't open without his permission. He placed one hand on the handle and glanced at Loki who nodded.

"Go ahead," Loki said. "Open it."

CHAPTER 11

William swung the door open and took a step back. Bradley, covered in blood, collapsed through the threshold onto the floor.

"Bradley!" Loki exclaimed as he rushed to his brother's side. He gently rolled Bradley onto his back. His eyes were bruised and swollen nearly shut; his nose was badly broken with fresh blood still pouring out of it. His cheeks were puffed out like hornet stings with open gashes. His right arm was broken, the lower bone slightly protruding through the skin. He trembled on the floor, coughing up blood and gargling between gasps. Everyone crowded his side.

"What happened?"

"Who did this?"

Various questions flooded the room as the group sprung into panic.

"Everyone calm down and back off!" Loki ordered. "Rayme, get me fresh towels from downstairs and something to stop the bleeding."

Rayme ran off down to the bar without hesitation. A large pool of blood was quickly forming beneath Bradley's battered body. He was losing too much blood too fast, barely clinging to life. The metallic smell of blood filled the air and stung Jule's nostrils. She covered her nose with the sleeve of her hoodie trying to avoid the powerful smell.

"I need a belt!" Loki ordered through sobs as he positioned his wounded brother in the middle of the room. Demonik quickly removed his leather belt and handed it to Loki.

"William, shut the door." Loki's orders were much quieter now. Everyone was silent, frozen, watching in shock and dismay.

"Bradley, this is going to hurt, but I have to try to reset your arm," Loki said softly to his whimpering brother. Bradley nodded slowly and turned his head away, preparing himself for the pain. *SNAP!* Loki forced the bones back into their place and held Bradley's arm firmly.

As soon as William closed the door, there came a knock. Rayme rushed in with the towels, promptly wrapping the broken arm around a short towel rod and fastening it tight with the belt.

"Do you have something for the bleeding?" Loki asked.

"Oh, yes, in my bag." Rayme rushed to his bag removing a jar of herbs. Clumping a handful of the pungent herb in his mouth, he chewed it up quickly then wadded it up into little portions and began applying small heaps of the masticated herb to each open wound. Loki took a handful and copied Rayme's example. As Rayme chewed the herb, he lifted Bradley's shirt for a more thorough investigation of his injuries.

"He has substantial bruising around his ribs," he noted to Loki. "And here, around his kidneys." Rayme pointed to dark blue and purple discoloration that spread over Bradley's skin.

"That's bad," Loki frowned. "He's bleeding internally."

Bradley suddenly began convulsing violently on the floor, coughing and spewing up blood.

"He's going into shock!" Rayme declared.

"Put this towel in his mouth and help me hold him still!" Loki demanded.

William, Athan, and Demonik quickly followed the demand and held Bradley down firmly on the floor as best they could. Rayme placed a washrag in Bradley's mouth to prevent him from breaking his teeth or biting off his tongue during his convulsions. Bradley's body writhed and jerked on the floor. With a deep gasp, his eyes opened as wide as the swelling would allow them to, his body went rigid and then suddenly limp, his eyes rolling back into his head and one last breath escaping his lips with a bubble of blood.

"Bradley! Bradley, wake up! Come on, stay with me!" Loki cried, desperately shaking his brother's shoulders, lightly slapping his cheeks in an attempt to wake him. There was no response. Bradley lay limp on the floor, his breathing ceased.

Sobs erupted in the room. Jule's hands trembled at her sides as tears rolled down her cheeks dripping on the floor.

"Bradley, no," Loki whimpered. William put his arm around his grieving friend. Loki burst into tears, scooping up Bradley into his lap and rocking back and forth with his lifeless brother cradled in his arms.

"Why you?" he sobbed.

"What do we do now?" Catarina asked quietly, tears steadily flowing from her eyes.

"We have to do something!" Azul demanded. "Our friend was just killed and you know it was them. You know it was the Order!"

"We should hunt them down. Right now!" declared Viktor with a slam of his fist on a desk. Jule jumped at the sudden loud bang.

Demonik sat silently, staring at his dead friend, his face expressionless and numb. Catarina approached him, climbing into his lap, wrapping her arms around his neck and resting her head against his.

Jule couldn't believe this was happening, her friend dead, lifeless, covered in blood on the floor right in front of her! She shook with fear, her entire body trembling. Everything was *too* real. Her life was in danger. All of their lives were in danger. What could she do? She was useless and helpless, unable to transform, unable to do anything. She could be an easy target.

Esadora clung onto Jule's arm, worried and shook. She held her friend as they wept together.

"Let me think. We-we can't do anything rash," Loki stammered.

"Are you kidding me? 'Can't do anything rash'? Loki, your brother is dead!" Azul challenged, jumping up angrily from his seat.

"I know!"

"Then let's go kill these bastards!" Azul roared, raising his arms up like a warrior primed for battle.

"We don't even know where they are, or who they are, or how many there are. It would be foolish to retaliate right now," Loki rationalized through his tears.

William stood up to challenge Azul. Standing a full head taller than Azul, he attempted to intimidate with his size, but Azul never let his height play a factor in any brawl. He was fearless and he was careless, often blindly getting into fights and just as often losing, but never learning. William stood tall, glaring into Azul's eyes, daring him to make a move.

"Don't be foolish, snake," William said sternly.

"Back off dog, I'll rip you in half!" Azul growled through is teeth.

Demonik approached his brother and tugged him away from the potential conflict.

"Not now," he whispered in Azul's ear.

Azul growled and glared at William who simply shot a snide, challenging smile in retort.

"I don't need this right now – you two better knock it off," Loki demanded. "We need to take care of Bradley. I need help bringing him home and cleaning him up." He sniffled and wiped his nose, smearing his brother's blood over his mouth. "Someone also needs to help me clean this place up, please."

"I'll stay and clean," Jule quietly offered.

"I will too," added Esadora.

"I'll help you with Bradley," said Rayme.

"Me too," William said softly.

"I'll help with Brad," Athan added, again quietly repeating his statement to himself.

"What are *you* going to do?" Loki directed his question to the gang on the couch.

Azul and Demonik exchanged glances. Viktor sat perched like a gargoyle on the arm of the couch, his long trench coat draping on the floor. His mischievous eyes gleamed.

"I have to get back to work," Azul grumbled.

"I just want to go home," Catarina whispered, her soft voice trembling.

"I'll take Cat home. Viktor, do you want to ride with us? And I'll drop you off at work, Azul," said Demonik, his voice robotic and void of emotion.

"Alright then."

"Fidelia, what are you going to do?" Esadora asked, concerned.

Fidelia was silent for a moment, staring off into space. She appeared to be in shock. Rayme made his way over to her and held her in a long embrace, attempting to bring her comfort. Tears finally released and flowed from her emerald green eyes. She sobbed hard with her face buried into Rayme's arms.

"Come on, let's go outside," he said as he led her past the pool of blood, careful not to step in it. They disappeared out the door. The room fell silent; a thickness loomed in the air.

Viktor leapt off his perch and signaled the rest to follow. The small group said their goodbyes and headed out of the building. In the silence, Jule heard the sound of car doors outside opening and shutting, the rev of a small engine as a vehicle took off down the road. Then, they were gone.

"William, we need to keep an eye on them. I'm afraid one of them is going to do something reckless," Loki broke the silence.

William nodded expressing the same concern.

"Actually, there's something I've been meaning to tell you," Jule said quietly.

Loki looked up from his brother. "Go on," he said.

"The other night, after Jeff's funeral, I overheard Viktor talking to Azul on the phone. He said something about their time coming soon. I couldn't hear everything he said, but it sounded like they might be planning something."

"Great." William rolled his eyes.

"Why didn't you tell me this before?" Loki demanded.

"I don't know," she stammered. "There's been a lot going on." She sheepishly looked down at the floor with guilt.

"It's okay," Loki said quietly. "We have to keep an eye on them, but we also have to be on alert about the Order."

Jule looked down at Bradley's body, still protectively cradled in Loki's lap on the floor, the deep red blood glistening in the light. She wept. Esadora held her gently as she cried uncontrollably from grief and fear alike.

"I think you should take Jule back to your ranch," Loki suggested.

Jule quickly raised her head from Esadora's shoulder.

"No!" she exclaimed. "There was something out there – what if we were followed? It's not safe out there!" Jule began to panic remembering the odd scent William picked up, the ominous atmosphere she experienced. She had a gut feeling that they were followed and didn't want to ignore it.

"Hey it's fine. My ranch is out in the middle of nowhere and if anything happens I can handle it," William urged.

"There was something out there? You didn't tell me this," Loki said, annoyed.

"It's nothing. I just smelled something I didn't recognize, that's all."

Loki frowned. William's attempt at reassurance wasn't too convincing.

"His ranch is the best place for you to be, honestly. It's away from town and out of the way. I think it's safer than staying here," he finally agreed after contemplating their limited options.

"Well, what about the rest of you? You guys are in town, it won't be safe, will it?" questioned Jule.

"My house is very secure; I've set it up to be that way," Loki answered. "Anyone who wishes to stay with me is welcome to. I have plenty of room. I urge those of you who are helping me with my brother to stay. The more of us that are there the better our odds will be if something were to happen."

Esadora, Fidelia, and Athan all nodded

"What about the others?" William asked as he gestured out the window, signifying the group that departed.

"I'm going to try to persuade them to stay at my house. I think I can convince Demonik and he can maybe talk to the others. Catarina will follow him anywhere, so if we have Demonik there then we're almost guaranteed to have her as well. It's Azul and Viktor that are going to be more difficult to convince. I just hope they don't do anything stupid tonight."

Loki took a deep breath, wiping away his last tears with his blood-covered hands. He gently laid his brother on the floor with care and slowly stood up weakly, finding the wall to lean on for support.

"We need to deal with this now," Loki said to the floor, unable to look up from his head-rush. "William, I've got it from here. You just take Jule and get out of here, okay?"

"What are you going to do with Bradley?" Jule asked.

"As much as I would like to lay my brother to rest, it's clearly not a good idea to perform a funeral right now. We will have our time to grieve and pay our due respects, but for now I must preserve his body and keep it safe." Loki's voice shook with frustration as he spoke. "We need to be vigilant and cautious, bringing no unnecessary attention to ourselves until this issue is resolved."

William nodded and led Jule with his arm around her down the stairs to the lot in the back of the building. Jule's eyes were still wide with fear, darting this way and that, searching for danger that could be lurking around any corner.

"Calm down," William coaxed, feeling her on edge. "I won't let anything happen to you. I promise."

He stopped and lifted Jule's chin to give her a light, loving kiss.

"Do you need to get anything or are you ready to go now?" he asked.

"I should probably get some things from Lillith's house. And drop my car off. Can you take me out to your ranch? I don't think I could drive all that way," Jule admitted.

"Of course. I'll follow you to Lillith's house, make sure you get there okay."

William escorted Jule to her vehicle then jogged to his truck parked five spaces away. Jule pulled out onto the road and headed to Lillith's. Her white-knuckled hands shook on the steering wheel, her vision blurred through the tears. It was a long, dreary drive.

MORE THAN HUMAN

CHAPTER 12

Lillith was standing outside waiting for Jule. She approached her car as William pulled up behind and parked in the driveway.

"Loki called me and told me what happened," Lillith explained as Jule got out of the car. They hugged each other tightly. "Are you guys okay?"

Jule's hands were finally at ease and stopped shaking. The tears in her eyes dried and she regained her composure.

"Yeah, we're fine," Jule replied with a hard gulp. "I'm going with William out to his ranch tonight. Will you and the kids be safe here?"

"I have kept us off of the radar pretty well so I'm not too worried," Lillith said with firm confidence.

William got out of his truck and approached them, finding his place next to Jule and resting his arm protectively around her shoulders. Lillith smiled sweetly at their affection. Jule wrapped her arm around his waist and rested her head against his chest.

"We're just here to get some of her things," William explained.

Jule released her grasp and headed up to the guest house to gather her belongings. She snagged up her old backpack dumping out its current contents and placed a clean change of clothes, a few hygienic items, her phone, and charger.

William and Lillith were chatting as Jule returned ready to go.

"You keep her safe," Lillith demanded motherly.

"I will," he promised.

Jule loaded herself into William's truck and waved goodbye as they headed out. She worried for her friend and her children.

Stay safe, she silently wished them.

William rested his hand in Jule's lap as they drove. She placed her hand on his and they clasped together in a firm hold. She gazed out the window at the hypnotic passing streetlights, the hum of the engine deafening in the silence.

William turned on the stereo. They listened to the music without saying a word all the way to the ranch. After some time, he pulled up the dark driveway and parked in front of the house.

"I'll show you the bedroom so you can set your stuff down," he said as Jule followed him inside. He turned a few lights on his way through the house to the spiral staircase. It was roomy up there with a cozy little reading hut tucked away in a niche framed with a small bookshelf and a white-framed window. Jule imagined herself sitting in that spot reading a book and drinking hot coffee on a cold rainy day. *What a perfect little spot,* she thought with delight. She followed him down a short hallway to the last door on the left. A king size bed with log poles making up the frame sat in the middle of the opposite wall. A massive black and red comforter draped over the mattress nearly reached the floor. Pillows of all sizes were stacked neatly at the head of the bed. A Navajo rug that matched the bedding set hung behind it on the wall. To the left of the bed was a floor-to-ceiling pair of glass doors with elegant silver handles that opened up to a large balcony overlooking the national forest. Jule took in her surroundings and admired the room. Judging from how beautiful the rest of the house was, she expected nothing less.

"Wow that's a really nice bed," Jule complimented as she tossed her things down carelessly on the floor by the nightstand, "Looks really comfy."

"Want to try it out?" William teased with a wink trying to lighten the mood.

Jule blushed and shied away. She opened one of the great glass doors and stepped out onto the balcony. The moon, in its last night of being full, shone high above. The grass below glistened with dew in the starlight, swaying to-and-fro in the breeze like a green lake rippling on the shore. She listened intently to the night, absorbing the sounds of the crickets, the night birds, and the wind bustling through the trees for any sign of danger. She strained her weak eyes in the night, surveying the area below, but she saw nothing.

William approached from behind, gently running his hand over her back as he stood next to her. He peered out over the landscape scanning the tree line.

"Can you see anything?" Jule whispered.

"No."

"Can you smell anything?"

"No," he said again. "You can relax. We are fine here, I'm sure of it." He grabbed Jule gently and turned her towards him, looking her deep into her eyes. "I'll protect you."

Jule stood up on her toes to kiss him.

"So what do you want to do? I could grab a blanket and we could head down to the field and build a fire again, sit under the moonlight," he suggested.

"That sounds nice," Jule said dreamily as she imagined falling asleep wrapped in his arms next to the fire under the stars. The idea was the epitome of a romantic date in Jule's mind, absolutely perfect.

"I have some wine, too," William said with a wink.

"Oh really, well I guess now we're all set." Jule smiled.

They headed back downstairs gathering two warm blankets, two wine glasses, and the bottle of wine. William removed a rifle mounted above the door as they stepped outside and brought it with him.

"Just in case," he added, holding up the rifle.

The night air had a brisk chill to it. A few puffy clouds, faintly visible, lingered about in the sky slowly drifting by. The moonlight peeked out from behind the clouds brightly illuminating the grassy fields for a moment before cowering behind another, returning the world to darkness. Jule's tired, blurry eyes made it difficult for her to see where she was going. She made sure to follow close behind William as he guided her with his hand safely through to the clearing. They placed their things inside the dirt circle and laid out the blanket on the ground.

"I'll go get some more wood and start a fire," said William as he trotted off back in the direction of the house.

Jule sat down on the blanket, taking care not to knock over and break the wine glasses. She pulled out the wine opener from her pocket and struggled to open the bottle. Finally, she forcefully managed to pop the cork, spilling a bit of the red wine onto the blanket. *Shit,* she thought embarrassed at her clumsiness. *I've ruined the blanket. Maybe he won't notice.* She positioned herself onto the painfully noticeable red spot on the blue blanket to conceal it, not caring whether her pants stained or not, and poured two generous glasses of wine. William trotted back cradling some lumber in his arms and carefully dropped it into a pile next to the pit. He knelt down and began placing the wood over a small bundle of kindling and ignited it, bringing a warm orange glow to the chilly summer night.

William draped the second blanket over them as he took a seat next to Jule. She handed him his glass of wine and they clinked their glasses together in a toast before gulping down the sweet, dry beverage. Sitting together in silence, holding each other, they simply enjoyed the moment. Jule could feel William's body heat radiate from his torso, his intoxicating musk lingered into her nostrils making her feel almost as if she was drugged. She laid her head against his shoulder and he turned and kissed her forehead. He made her feel safe and secure; appreciated and loved. She never wanted it to end.

"I have to pee," Jule said, a little embarrassed, as she stood up scoping out an appropriate place to relieve herself.

"There's not much around here but there's a few bushes over there." William pointed in the opposite direction of the house. "Or you can use the bathroom."

Not wanting to trek all the way back, Jule clumsily stumbled through the dark towards the bushes. She could hardly see where she was going. As she got closer, Jule was finally able to make out the shrubs and squatted down behind them. Lacking toilet paper, Jule searched with her hands through the grass until she felt the familiar long, thick fuzzy leaves of a mullein plant. She removed a few of the leaves and used them to wipe herself, tossing it as far away from her as she could when she finished.

As Jule stood up to fasten her pants the campfire returned to view. She expected to see William sitting near it, maybe poking at the fire with a stick, but he was nowhere to be found. She began to panic and ran back to the fire nervously, searching for signs of him.

"William?" she called out. "William, where are you?"

She looked for the rifle he had brought, but it was missing, too.

"William!" she shouted. "This isn't funny! Come out!"

A wave of worry swept over Jule as the dark night replied with nothing but eerie silence. Even the crickets and birds had ceased their nighttime music. She felt uneasy – something was amiss. Quickly, she darted off back to the house, running as fast as her feeble legs could carry her. She needed to call someone for help. Suddenly, she felt a prick in her neck and she stopped dead in her tracks. Confused, she reached up to the back of her neck where the pain was stemming from and felt something hard and plastic. She removed the object and studied it in her hand; it was a tranquilizer dart of some kind. Her vision began to blur and spin. Her head felt loopy and she collapsed to the ground finding her body paralyzed and unable to move. Through her blurred, fading vision she saw three fuzzy black figures standing over her, peering down at her. Her world went dark as she passed out.

MORE THAN HUMAN

CHAPTER 13

Pain shot through Jule's head as she regained consciousness; the effects of the drug that was pumped into her bloodstream still lingering. She strained to open her eyes. The sunrise, with its blinding pink and orange light, peaked over the hill. She struggled to her feet, her body sore from lying on rocks and sticks for hours throughout the night. Still in a haze, she took in her surroundings and tried piecing together her broken memory. She remembered being with William by the fire, and then having to pee.

"Oh no, William!" Panic swept through her again as she wasted no time in rushing back to the house. She burst in through the back door and frantically began searching for a phone.

"The kitchen," she said to herself as she darted towards it.

A phone hung on the wall just inside the kitchen across from the sink. Jule grabbed the phone and immediately started punching in Loki's phone number memorized by heart. Not a single signal came from the phone. Not even the beeps from the buttons on the pad made any response. Irritated, Jule slammed the phone back into its place and began searching for her cell phone. She recalled leaving it on the coffee table in the living room and rushed to it, finding it smashed in pieces on the floor instead.

"There's got to be another phone in this house!" she cried out in frustration.

Jule frantically searched in every room, but each phone she found was just as dead as the first. She flipped a light switch on the wall of the bedroom but the light gave no response. Angrily, she flipped the switch off and on again, expecting that maybe if she did it enough times, the light would magically respond and turn on. Nothing happened.

"Shit, they must have cut the power to the whole house," she mumbled to herself. "I've got to get out of here!"

Deciding to drive back to town, Jule sped down the stairs out to William's truck, only to find the tires slashed and the engine wires cut. The truck was going nowhere.

"Fuck!" she shouted and began to cry. *What am I going to do? I have no vehicle, no way to contact anyone, and I'm out in the middle of nowhere,* she thought dismally to herself. The only thing Jule could think to do was to walk back to town. She quickly ran inside, grabbing her backpack and some water, and then headed out on her long journey.

The early morning sun warmed her chilled bones as she walked with a quick pace down the driveway to the main dirt road. Her body and head still ached as the drugs continued wearing off, but she pushed herself forward regardless. Jule shielded her eyes with her hand as she looked at position of the sun to get a sense of time, though she was more guessing than anything. *I think it's been a few hours already.* She frowned and concentrated back on her task. Racing against time she quickened her pace, fighting through the throbbing pain in her head and aches in her legs to make it back and find William.

As Jule rounded a corner in the road, the rumbling sound of an old truck approached from behind. Jule threw herself into some bushes to the side of the road. *Someone from the Order must have still been around William's house. I wasn't careful enough,* Jule thought, punishing herself for her carelessness. The noisy truck slowed as it got nearer to where Jule abandoned the road for cover and pulled over, the brakes screeching as it came to a halt. The exhaust rumbled noisily. The foul fumes rose into Jule's nose, making her gag. She hunkered down lower as she heard the driver's side door creak open and feet hit the gravel, crunching as they approached. *Shit, they saw me.* Jule's heart raced. She balled up her fists and swallowed hard.

A twig snapped right in front of the bush she was hiding in as a brown, worn cowboy boot came into view. Jule's eyes darted up, peering through the foliage to a figure standing before her. She jumped up quickly to surprise her attacker. An elderly Navajo man stumbled back and grabbed at his chest, startled. Jule immediately realized her mistake.

"Are you okay, Miss?" the man asked, concerned.

"Oh, yes, I'm fine. I'm sorry I didn't mean to scare you," she replied, standing behind the bush.

"Do you need a ride into town?"

Jule looked around nervously, feeling uneasy. Normally, she wouldn't get into a vehicle with a stranger in the middle of nowhere, but her options were limited and she needed to get help. She took a deep breath, her gut telling her to take the chance. He seemed harmless enough.

"Yes, please," she said as she came out from her cover.

"Well, get in then," the old man instructed as he climbed back in his truck.

Jule's short legs struggled to climb into the lifted Bronco. She slammed her door shut and strapped on her seat belt. Her hands fidgeted nervously in her lap.

"Name is Jacob."

"Jule," she answered quietly. "Nice to meet you."

The old man glanced down, noticing Jule's anxious trembling.

"You cold?" he asked and turned on the heat.

Jule said nothing as she rubbed her hands in front of the warm air emitting from the dashboard.

"What are you doing out here? Are you by yourself?"

"I was, uh, camping with a friend of mine." She was careful not to divulge too much information to this strange, but kind man.

"Well, where's your friend? Did they leave you?" he pressed on.

"He had to go somewhere. My truck broke down and I have no phone so I had to walk back to town," she partially lied.

"That's a really long way to walk. Glad I found ya when I did. There's lions out here and all sorts of dangerous stuff," he rambled on.

Jule nodded her head and stared out the window. She felt like she was going to jump out of her own skin. *We need to hurry, old man.* He wasn't driving fast enough and her impatience grew by the minute.

"It's nice to meet another kin in this area."

Jule was confused – she was in no way possibly related to this man, so how could they be "kin"?

"What do you mean?"

The old man chuckled.

"You're a lycanthrope, ain't ya?"

Jule looked up at the old man, his face wise with wrinkles. His dark skin was baked by the sun. Two long, thick black braids with beaded eagle feathers decorating the ends hung over each shoulder.

"Well, kind of I guess. How did you know?" She raised an eyebrow.

"I can smell it in your blood," he simply answered.

"Are you a lycan too?"

"No," he laughed. "But I'm a cousin to the lycans. I'm a skin-walker."

"I have never heard of a skin-walker. What is that?" Jule felt more relaxed now in his presence, her curiosity peaking.

"In my culture, we are highly feared. We're seen as evil, but we're really not. Skin-walkers have the ability to shape shift. Legend became that skin-walkers killed their victims and then wore their skins, but we don't. I don't know how that legend got started, but ever since then, my species has had a hell of a time trying to survive. Try being Indigenous *and* a skin-walker, you have very few allies."

"That's too bad," Jule said softly.

"Yeah it is. So where do you want me to drop you off in town? Do I need to take you to a mechanic? If so I got a buddy who…"

"No, just take me downtown please," Jule interrupted.

The old man nodded his head and focused his eyes back on the road. The dirt road ended as they finally hit the pavement and Jule's heart pounded hard. They weren't too far away now, but Jule couldn't get there quick enough. Every possible terrible scenario played through her mind of what could be happening to her love. *I hope I make it in time.*

She leapt out of the truck as soon as it pulled up in front of L&B Bar, kindly thanked the man, and hurried to the door of the bar. Desperately she pulled at every knob only to discover each door to the building was locked tight; no one was there.

"Jule!" a voice called from across the street. Jule spun around towards the voice and saw Esadora jogging up to her.

"Esadora, I need your help," she said frantically.

Esadora's eyes widened.

"What's wrong?"

"William was kidnapped last night from the ranch. I was drugged with a tranquilizer and left behind. I need to find him," Jule pleaded.

"Where do we start looking?" she asked as she guided Jule down the street to her parked gold Nissan car.

"I –I don't know," Jule admitted as she got in. "I have no idea where they took him." Tears formed in her eyes.

"Who took him?" Esadora asked.

"I don't know, I didn't see their faces, but there were three of them." Jule paused for a moment trying hard to remember any helpful details. An idea popped into her head.

"Wait, Loki told me about your ability. Can you use your spirit immersion to find him?" she asked, hopeful.

Esadora frowned.

"I'm not well trained or practiced in it; I'm still learning."

"Can't you try? Please?" Jule begged.

Esadora took a deep sigh before answering.

"Yeah, I can try, but we should go to my house to do it. No one should bother us there, we'll have privacy so I can concentrate better," she said as she carefully pulled away from the curb and headed home.

"Thank you so much!" Jule exclaimed, tears rushing down her face.

Esadora drove as quickly as she could. Luckily she lived only a few blocks away, but then again, everything was close by in this small town. They arrived at a small blue and white house with a short chain-link fence enclosing it. They hurried into the house. Jule tossed her stuff on the floor as she walked in and closed the door behind her.

"Lock the door, please," Esadora requested as she closed the drapes to the windows and drew the blinds shut. She pushed aside the coffee table in the tiny living room and laid out a tie-dye blanket, sitting cross legged in the very center.

"What do I need to do?" Jule asked impatiently.

"I need you to be still and quiet," instructed Esadora. She closed her eyes and slowed her breathing. Jule plopped down on the floor where she was standing and watched her friend try to perform a miracle.

"I can't promise this will work," she said softly.

"I know, and I thank you for trying."

Jule sat intently studying her, having no idea what to expect. Esadora breathed deeply and slowly, her hands resting gently on her knees. Her back was straight and her shoulders were relaxed. Her head pointed down to her lap. Without warning, Esadora fell onto the floor, her eyes rolling into the back of her head, her skin dulling with the absence of her spirit. Suddenly, her body began convulsing and jerking, tears streaming from her eyes. Horrified, Jule scrambled to her friend's side and held her shaking head in her hands. Esadora's arms and legs thrashed about violently. With a gasp, Esadora sat up and screamed, frantically feeling her legs and arms with her hands, her eyes wide with terror, her color slowly returning to normal. She buried her face in Jule's chest. Jule wrapped her arms around her friend, rocking her back and forth trying to soothe her.

"You're okay," she insisted. "You're safe, Esadora."

Jule lifted her friend's chin with her index finger to look her in the eyes.

"What happened?"

Esadora silenced her cries and wiped away her tears.

"I saw –I saw what they were doing to him," she stuttered.

"You found William? Where is he? What's happening?" Jule bombarded Esadora with questions.

"He's somewhere dark," she began explaining. "There's dirt everywhere and it felt cold. He's in pain – he's in so much pain," she began sobbing again. "Blood everywhere, a knife, a woman I've never seen before with two men, that's all I could see. It was horrible!" She covered her face with her hands.

"Do you know where that is?" Jule pressed, holding Esadora's shoulders firmly.

"I –I think they're in the old mines." Esadora looked up into Jule's eyes, shining with intense urgency.

"I need your car," Jule said.

Esadora nodded and handed over her keys.

"Be careful Jule," she pleaded.

"I will," she uncertainly promised.

Jule hugged Esadora once more before running back to the car.

CHAPTER 14

Jule pulled up to the dirt lot at the entrance of the path to the mine and spotted a light brown SUV clumsily hidden behind a short, fat juniper tree. She stopped the car behind it, slowly getting out, investigating the suspicious vehicle. Peering through the windows, she saw nothing of use; it was empty.

She sprinted as fast as she could down the long dirt path in search of William, her heart pounding hard in her chest, adrenaline pulsing through her veins. She stopped short at the mouth of the dark cave, looking down into its depths, hoping she was at the right place and that she was on time. *Hang on William, I'm coming.* Carefully, she made her descent down the steep, rocky entrance and cautiously ventured further into the cold cave, the light fading, leaving her alone in darkness. Her eyes strained to adjust to no avail. She blindly navigated her way through the pitch black by feeling along the walls with her hands and slowly shuffling her feet across the dirt floor. Minutes agonizingly passed by as she made her way deeper into the cavern.

The soft orange glow of a fire appeared from around the corner down a tunnel to her left. *There they are,* she hopefully thought. The flickering, dancing light freed Jule from her blindness and she was finally able to see. She let go of the wall of the cave and crept closer quietly, hearing voices as she neared. The tunnel opened up into a great underground cavern, a fire in the center dancing away carrying the smoke up through a crack in the ceiling. Four figures then came into view, their shadows creeping on the walls as they moved, except for one. Jule could make out a body hanging at the end of long chains dangling down from the ceiling. Enormous silver hooks pierced deep in his back, thick drops of blood rhythmically splashing collected in a pool beneath him. William hung naked and limp in his human form from the giant hooks, his head bowed down to his chest, unconscious. Near him sat a large steel table with a collection of various torture tools: blades, hooks, saws, all manner of sharp objects freshly used with deep red blood still coating them.

Jule crouched down behind a boulder trying to stay out of sight while she contemplated what to do. One of the figures –the shorter one – moved towards William and slapped him hard across the face. The blade of a knife shimmered in the figure's hand.

"Wake up!" a woman shouted. The voice was eerily familiar and Jule's hair raised.

Without thinking, she stood up and approached the woman.

"Annabelle?" her voice shook as she made her presence known.

Annabelle spun around and jumped back, surprised.

"Jule," she exclaimed quietly, "What are you doing here? You're not supposed to be here."

Annabelle lowered her knife, raising her free hand up to assure Jule that she meant no harm. The other two figures, as Jule could see them clearly now, were two very large and intimidating men. They started towards her as if to restrain her when Annabelle suddenly called them off. The men hesitated before complying with the order and stopped in their tracks, crossing their arms angrily.

"No," she said sharply to the men. "I will handle this." Annabelle turned back to Jule who stood with her mouth agape and eyes wide in surprise.

"Jule," she coaxed gently, "I'm not going to hurt you." She carefully placed the knife down on the table and raised both arms up, slowly approaching her.

Jule couldn't believe her eyes. Her best friend, the person she shared her most intimate secrets with and *trusted*, was impossibly standing before her.

"What- what are you doing?" Jule stammered through her confusion, her eyes darting between her best friend and her tortured soulmate who hung helplessly bleeding out from the enormous hooks.

"I'm sorry you had to find out this way, but I am just doing my job. You see, I am a Hunter and this is my prey," Annabelle said nonchalantly as she gestured her hand to William. "My job is to wipe out impurities and monsters like him. There's no place for them in this world. They're slowly becoming extinct and we are purifying the Earth."

"No!" Jule shouted. "Don't hurt him – I love him. Please, let him go!"

Annabelle scoffed.

"Oh, that's cute," she said condescendingly. "You love this filthy mutt?"

Annabelle began circling William's body, wandering to the display of torture devices, gently running her finger across them as she passed.

"I don't want to hurt you, Jule, so I am going to give you one chance. Leave now while you can. I know these things have been trying to convince you that you're one of them but you're not. We don't kill humans and I certainly don't want to kill my friend, but if you do not leave now I will have no other choice."

Jule firmly stood her ground. Her heart beat furiously as beads of sweat dripped down her temple, her fists tightly clenched at her sides, her nails digging into the palms of her hands.

"But, how... *why* are you here? Have you been following me?" she asked angrily.

"Yes," Annabelle answered without hesitation.

"For how long?" Jule demanded.

"Since we met." Annabelle paused and looked down at the ground before continuing, as if she felt shame in her admittance. "My parents are members of The Order of Purity. They, too, are Hunters. Many years ago, your family name raised a red flag in our division and we were assigned to track and monitor you, waiting to see if you were a potential threat. I was tasked with befriending you and getting close to you, which wasn't very hard and I rather enjoyed the friendship we created, if I'm being honest. When I am done here, I will be reporting back to The Order, removing you from the red flag list and we will have to assign a sweep team to the area to clean up the rest of these filth." She paused again, taking a deep breath. "I am your friend, Jule, and I'm sorry you had to see this."

"Are you the one who killed Bradley?"

Annabelle frowned.

"If you're asking if he died by my hand, he did not. I liked him, he was sweet." She briefly smiled ever so slightly. "His death was unfortunate, however. My men got a little carried away while interrogating him about your little group of friends."

A fury of conflicting emotions swept over Jule. Here was her best friend – her *childhood* friend – torturing the love of her life and was responsible for the murder of Bradley. All at once she felt rage, confusion, betrayal, and devastation. Accepting Annabelle's offer to simply turn around and leave William behind was not an option. She scanned the room absorbing her surroundings and tried to piece together the best way to get them out of there. The two large brutes stood to the side of the cavernous room, about twenty feet away from her. Annabelle still was directly in front of her, less than eight feet away. She glanced at the torture tools, but they were too far away to seriously consider. There was nothing Jule could see that she could use to her advantage and she began to feel helpless and defeated.

"Take her out of here," Annabelle ordered the men. "Goodbye Jule." She turned her back.

The large men quickly began to approach Jule, their arms outstretched and ready to snatch her. Her heart raced, sending a surge of electrifying adrenaline throughout her whole body. She let out a scream of rage and suddenly, miraculously, began rapidly transforming into her wolf form. Her size increased dramatically, ripping her clothes into a shredded pile on the ground. Her jaw lengthened into the canine's snout bearing a mouthful of sharp teeth, fur spread like wildfire across her entire body, her legs and arms lengthened as she fell forward onto the ground. Standing on all fours, she was at eye-level with the men who stopped abruptly a few feet from her and stared wide-eyed, frozen in terror.

Jule let out another intense roar before springing upon the two men, knocking them both down at once, digging her teeth and claws into their throats, spraying blood in either direction splattering the cavern walls.

Their blood dripped from the beast's jowls as she turned to meet eyes with Annabelle who looked upon her, eyes wide in horror. Annabelle carefully backed up, her hands rose defensively in front of her. Jule approached menacingly with a low growl, a fiery fury burning deep in her eyes.

"Please," Annabelle begged, her voice shaking. "Please don't do this. I'll leave, right now. I'll get out of here and you two will never see me again."

Jule hesitated for a moment, wanting so much to believe her friend, but deep in her heart she knew that she couldn't trust Annabelle and she couldn't risk allowing her to escape. She had to protect William and her other friends by any means necessary.

Like a flash of lightning, Jule leapt forward onto Annabelle and swiftly bit down on her throat. Annabelle didn't have a chance to react before Jule's jaws found and pierced her jugular. Blood gurgled out of her mouth and gaping holes on either side of her throat as she tried to speak. Her head rocked to the side as she lay lifeless, blood steadily flowing onto the ground.

Jule, panting heavily, stepped back and looked down at the body, giving a hard nudge with her nose. The body gave no response, confirming that Jule had killed the threat. She turned back towards William and trotted up to him. Positioning herself underneath him, she attempted to relieve the weight of his body from the hooks and supporting him on her back. William mumbled something incoherent, too weak to be able to speak. His breaths were slow and shallow. Blood still steadily dripping from his wounds onto Jule's back, staining her brown fur. She could feel he was slipping away. She whined frantically as she didn't know what else she could do to help him. She knew she needed to return to her human form, but her adrenaline rush prevented her from calming her mind enough to do so. She was still on edge and needed to be ready to fight off the next threat if one happened to appear.

The scent of blood was so heavy in the air that it was making her feel nauseous. The fire began to die out, filling the cave with smoke, burning her eyes. The sound of footsteps quickly approaching the cavern sent her hackles up. She leaned back onto her haunches, preparing to pounce on the intruders and defend her love. Suddenly, Loki and Rayme appeared in the dull light of the dying fire, Esadora trailing behind them carrying a duffel bag.

"It's okay, Jule, we're here to help," Loki coaxed gently as he slowly approached her. "Rayme, help me get him down," he directed as he made his way to William's side, wrapping his arms around his limp legs to lift him up. Jule side-stepped out of their way and sat down next to Esadora, watching carefully.

Rayme positioned himself opposite of Loki and raised William up, the hooks sliding out of the wounds. William immediately let out a cry of agony before losing consciousness once again. They sat William down on the ground and Rayme cradled him in his arms.

"Grab the blanket from the duffel bag and lay it out," Rayme said. He pulled his shoulder pack off and sat it down in front of him, rummaging through the contents with one hand and gently holding William with the other. Loki spread out the blanket and assisted Rayme in placing William upon it. Rayme removed a couple jars of herbs from his pack and a vial of some dark liquid and quickly began applying them to William's wounds, then bandaging them with cloth. By the time he was done, William's body was nearly completely covered with bandages.

"These silver hooks they used are inhibiting William's ability to heal," Rayme remarked with concern.

"Will he make it?" Loki asked.

"I don't know," he replied with a frown. "We'll just have to wait and see."

As Rayme continued tending to William, Loki walked up to Jule and knelt down in front of her. He gently stroked the fur on her shoulder, trying to keep her calm and relaxed. She looked down at him and rested her enormous head on his shoulder, tears dripping from her eyes as she pathetically whimpered.

"We need you to change back now, Jule," he said quietly in her ear. "I need you to concentrate on doing that. Focus on your human form and *will* yourself to become that." He then returned to Rayme, leaving Jule with Esadora.

"I have clothes for you," Esadora said as she removed them from the bag.

Jule nodded her head, then closed her eyes and envisioned herself standing before a mirror. She imagined her reflection, her light brown hair, her tan, freckled skin, her short stature, and her gray-blue eyes. Her wolf form slowly began to recede, transforming her back into her fragile, naked human self.

Esadora helped Jule get back into her clothes. She broke down into tears, covering her face with her hands and sobbing heavily as Esadora wrapped her arms around her. Sitting together on the ground, Esadora rocked Jule gently back and forth to comfort her. Jule succumbed to the exertion of her overwhelming transformation and fainted in Esadora's arms.

CHAPTER 15

Jule awoke to find herself comfortably tucked in a bed. She stirred, stretching her tired limbs and rubbing her sleepy eyes. When she looked around the room, it was unfamiliar to her. She had never been there before, but she recognized the smell of the house itself – she was in William's home. Quiet voices came from outside of the door, a mumbled conversation that she couldn't quite hear. She noticed that the blood from her victims had been cleaned from her hair and body, though some remained under her fingernails. Flashes of the mutilation performed with her own teeth and claws, her victim's terrified expressions as blood was spewing this way and that, began displaying in Jule's mind like a morbid slideshow. She shook her head hard, trying to erase the images from her mind. She could still taste them in her mouth.

Jule got up from the bed and went to the adjoining bathroom, turning on the faucet and rigorously scrubbing her hands and washing out her mouth. She grabbed a toothbrush and furiously brushed with far too much toothpaste, ignoring the common courtesy of not using someone's oral hygiene items. She desperately needed to get that horrible taste out of her mouth. Her stomach grumbled painfully with hunger. She dried her hands on a towel and made her way out the bedroom door.

Loki and Rayme were sitting on the couch in the living room deep in conversation when Jule came down the stairs.

"Jule, how are you feeling?" Loki asked as he stood up to get a better look at her.

"I'm sore and hungry," she said with a yawn.

"We made some breakfast earlier, there's still some left if you want some." Loki gestured towards the kitchen in offering.

"Yeah, that sounds good." Jule was absolutely famished. Her stomach growled angrily again. She gathered up the remaining scrambled eggs and sausage onto a plate and rejoined her friends in the living room.

"Wow, I've never seen you eat that much," Rayme chuckled. "You've got quite the appetite this morning."

"What time is it?" Jule asked with a mouthful of food.

Loki turned his wrist and checked his watch.

"It's just after eleven; you slept for a long time. I bet you needed it."

Jule suddenly realized that William wasn't in the room. She panicked, fearing the worst.

"Where's William?" she exclaimed. "Is he okay?"

"Calm down, Jule," said Rayme. "He's resting upstairs in the master bedroom. In fact, I should go check in on him."

"I want to see him," Jule said as she set her empty plate down on the coffee table in front of her.

"No, not yet, but I'll let you know when you can go in and see him. He needs some time to recover and so do you. Plus, I believe Loki has some things he would like to discuss with you."

Loki gave a nod as Rayme left the room and disappeared up the stairs. Jule fought off the urge to disobey Rayme's order and follow him anyway. She sat anxiously, fidgeting with her fingers in her lap.

"So, while you were spending time with William, I did a little digging and found out some interesting information about your family and your heritage," Loki said with a smile.

"Really, like what?" Jule asked. Her curiosity temporarily distracted her from her worries about William.

"Well, for starters, you are a descendant of one very powerful and important historical lycan. Your distant ancestor was the feared and respected Pirate Grace Benadette Foster, of the Foster Clan, a very prominent figure in lycan history." Loki paused for a moment.

"You, my dear," he continued. "Are the strongest lycan that exists, I believe. Your bloodline is a pure one, in a sense."

Jule was unsure how to handle this new information. She remembered her father talk about Grace a few times, but there was never any mention of her being a lycan or a pirate for that matter. Her father only spoke about how her ancestor was an explorer of sorts and how she never really settled down until very late in her life. He used it more as a guilt tactic to convince Jule to settle down, start a family, and marry early rather than just generally sharing family history. Jule didn't want to start a family or settle down until she had met the right person for her, so she empathized more with Grace than the point that her father tried to make.

"How did you find this out?"

"Athan has access to ancient records that were once thought to be lost. He collects information, family trees, lore, and legends. It's kind of his thing. He's like our record-keeper in a way. There were only a few documents on your family history – most of it was damaged and unreadable, but I was able to decipher the key points. I wish there was more I could tell you, but you truly possess such potential. Greatness flows in your veins, and I can't wait to help you tap into it." Loki grinned.

Jule smirked and began imagining her ancestor commanding an entire fleet of pirates and sailing tumultuous seas. *How fearless she must have been, how brave.*

Rayme returned down the stairs wiping the remnants of fresh blood off of his hands with a small towel.

"Is he okay?" Jule asked. "Can I see him now?"

"His wounds are not healing as quickly as they should. There may be some silver fragments from the hooks or other torture tools that were used on him floating around in his bloodstream. I don't possess the ability to remove them if there is. He's unconscious still, but I think it would be okay if you went in there."

Without hesitation, Jule stood up and briskly ran up the stairs. She stopped in her tracks just before the door, her hand trembling as she reached for the knob. She took a deep breath and headed in.

William was fast asleep in his bed. The blinds of the windows were closed most of the way, leaving the room fairly dark. She made her way quietly to his side, knelt down next to the bed and gently took his hand in hers. William took deep, struggling breaths, his chest quivering with each one. Jule squeezed his hand gently and pressed her lips on his wrist, giving him a soft kiss. Tears streamed down her cheeks as she looked him over and assessed his injuries. He was in bad shape.

Jule stayed in the room with William for hours, not wanting to leave his side in case he woke up. Loki entered to find that she had fallen asleep on the bed next to him. He lightly nudged her awake and asked that she come back downstairs. Reluctantly, she complied.

"It's going to be alright," he assured her. "Rayme is taking care of him."

"But he said himself that he's not sure if he can help William," she argued.

"Look, I trust Rayme with my life. I know he knows what he's doing; he doubts himself and his abilities too much. He truly is a gifted healer and William will pull through, it will just take some time. You need to be patient."

Jule grumbled under her breath. She was not a very patient person. She paced back and forth in frustration.

"I need to step outside. I need a smoke," she announced as she headed to the back porch, Loki trailing behind her.

Jule removed a cigarette from her pack and lit it, taking a long drag. She immediately spat the cigarette out in disgust and coughed hard.

"Ugh! This is horrible!" she exclaimed. "The smoke burns my nose and eyes and this thing tastes like it's been sitting in the rain for two weeks."

She crumpled up the rest of her pack and stomped it into the ground.

Loki began laughing.

"I was wondering when you were going to try that again," he said, still giggling.

"What?"

"You lycans are very sensitive to the toxins and chemicals in cigarettes, as you're just finding out. I wouldn't try smoking again."

"Well, that's one way to quit.".

"I will be staying here with you and William for the next few days. Rayme will be in and out to check on his condition."

"Wait, what about the mess down in the cave? What if someone finds the bodies? Will the police come looking for me?" Jule began to panic.

Loki leaned forward to rest his hand reassuringly on Jule's shoulder.

"You don't need to worry about that either, it's all taken care of," he said. "I sent a clean-up crew down there to remove the bodies and all evidence that any of us were down there. My crew was able to locate the hotel that the woman and her thugs were staying in. Lucky for us, the hotel room was paid for anonymously, so it was easy to close the account without raising any concern. As for the bodies, we will soon be reading in

118

the newspaper about the tragic accident where thieves looking to steal copper accidentally fell into the crusher at the mine." He leaned back against the porch railing and smirked with pride.

"Well, that's pretty clever," Jule complimented.

"I know," he said grinning wide. "We don't always get that lucky."

Loki's smile quickly vanished as he continued.

"However, the Order will notice their sudden disappearance and will send someone else to come investigate. We must be ready for when that happens."

MORE THAN HUMAN

CHAPTER 16

Nearly two weeks passed by before William finally began to show significant signs of recovery. Jule spent every moment she could by his side, helping Rayme tend to his wounds, change his bandages, and feed him when he was conscious.

In her spare time, while William slept, Jule continued practicing her transformations in the privacy of his land, finding it easier and more effortless to achieve the more she did it. She discovered that she could control her transformation by changing only a small part of herself at a time. She practiced growing out her claws while the rest of her body remained in human form. She focused her vision at night and was able to tap into the heightened senses of the wolf, making it easier to see in the dark, pick up the distant scent of a deer on the wind, or hear the snapping of a twig from a traveling pack of javelina a half-mile away. She was excited about her new-found abilities and impressed with herself at how quickly she was progressing. Jule learned on her own how to feel the energy of the moon at any time to give her the necessary power, finding that if the moon wasn't directly visible it took more concentration to accomplish the slightest change.

Loki peeked in the bedroom as Jule lie beside her love, her head resting on his shoulder as he slept.

"Hey, can I talk to you for a second?" Loki whispered.

Jule gave a nod and quietly exited the room, closing the door behind her and following Loki to the living room. They sat across from each other, Jule on the couch and Loki on a recliner. The mid-afternoon sun shone brightly through the windows behind Jule, illuminating Loki in a god-like way. His blond hair seemed to shimmer with gold in the light and his pale skin had a heavenly glow to it. He smiled brightly, clearly excited about something.

"I want to show you something spectacular tonight," he gleamed. "A very rare sight to see."

"What is it? I don't really want to leave William by himself; he's still too weak."

"That has already been arranged. Rayme will stay here to care for him while we are gone."

"You still haven't told me what it is you're even talking about," Jule pressed on.

Loki stood up from his seat and crossed the room to the window behind Jule and stared out into the lush woods across the grassy field.

"Do you know what tonight is?"

"Um, no, I don't. It's Friday?" Jule replied uncertainly.

"It's a new moon tonight."

"What happens on a new moon?"

"Azul shows his true self. Tonight, we will go to a discrete area in the woods where there is a large clearing and he will change, just as you can on a full moon. Though, what we will see him change into is not a wolf, but a dragon." His face gleamed as he turned to Jule. "Have you ever seen a dragon?"

"No, not that I am aware of," she giggled in response.

"I have to go for a bit, but I'll be back this evening to pick you up."

Loki gave Jule a hug before leaving the house. Jule sat back down on the couch in silence. The house was quiet. Occasionally, Jule could hear the wind pick up and sway a tree back-and-forth against the wall of the house, scraping and making small thuds. She finally got up from the couch and headed back to William's room. As she entered through the doorway, William was sitting up in bed cheerful and alert as she walked in.

"Hey there cutie-pants," he said pleasantly.

Jule blushed and smiled back at him, happy and relieved to see him awake and coherent.

"Hey, how are you feeling?" She crawled onto the bed and cuddled up beside him. William wrapped his right arm around her and gave her a light squeeze of affection.

"I'm better now that you're here with me."

Jule sniggered and blushed once again.

"Did I hear someone leave?" he asked her.

"Yeah, Loki just left. He wants to show me Azul's transformation tonight so Rayme is going to stay here with you while I'm gone."

"Awe, well, I'll miss you." William gave Jule a kiss on the forehead.

"I'll miss you too," she said softly, a hint of sorrow in her voice.

"What's wrong?"

"I'm worried." Jule frowned.

William sat upright in bed looking Jule straight in the eyes.

"Worried about what?"

"I'm worried that, like all of my previous relationships, this one will end, and that I'll lose you forever. You mean so much to me and I don't want to risk losing you." A tear danced in her eye.

William tenderly cupped her face in his hands and kissed her softly on the lips.

"You'll never lose me," he said as he wiped away her tear with his thumb, never letting go of her face. "Your other relationships failed because those other guys couldn't handle you. You're an intense person. But, you and I are the same. I know we're meant for each other, and now that I have you, I'm never letting you go. I love you."

MORE THAN HUMAN

CHAPTER 17

A knock on the door stirred William and Jule awake from their nap. Loki quietly walked in and apologized for the intrusion.

"It's time," he said to Jule. "Are you ready?"

Jule gave William a kiss before reluctantly leaving his side to stand up.

"Yeah, I guess so," she said with a yawn.

Rayme stepped into the room behind Loki.

"Don't worry about him, I'll be here. You go and have fun." He waved them off with his hand.

"Thanks," Jule said to Rayme.

Jule and William exchanged "I love yous" and waved goodbye. She followed Loki down the stairs and out the front door to his truck and got in, King and the other ravens cawing loudly at them from the top of the tree. The sun was nearly set, painting the sky with a brilliant arrangement of oranges and pinks. Jule stared daydreaming out the window as they drove in silence for about an hour before reaching their destination. The road wound up the mountain until they reached a large clearing the size of three football fields on the peak. Loki parked his truck next to a collection of other vehicles that Jule recognized. Most of the other group was already here, waiting.

Demonik, Azul, Catarina, and Viktor were gathered together in front of the vehicles laughing and talking with each other. Azul seemed to be the focus of their attention as he showed off to them with bragging stories of "kicking that guy's ass".

Athan, Fidelia, and Esadora were huddled among each other near the tree line engaged in their own, quiet conversation.

"The time is nearly upon us," Loki announced as he stepped away from his truck and approached, Jule closely following behind. The two cliques joined together in front of Loki as Jule went to Esadora's side. The girls greeted each other before turning their attention respectively back to Loki.

"It's nearly dark, are you ready Azul?" he asked.

Azul stepped forward and said something to Loki too quiet for Jule to hear, then turned away, walking past the group of spectators and disappeared into the tree line.

"He likes privacy while he undresses," Loki explained.

A few moments later, Azul stepped out from the cover of the trees and into the clearing of the meadow. Jule could hardly see him in the pitch black of night with her weak human eyes, so she tapped into her wolf's vision and his body became crystal clear in the dark. Everyone watched as his figure moved into the middle of the clearing. The cloudless night sky brilliantly glimmered with every visible star, planet, and astrological entity. Crickets chirped in harmony as the brisk wind picked up, stirring branches in the trees and whistling through the pines. A shiver ran down Jule's spine as she hugged her hoodie closer to her body.

Azul stretched his arms out, reaching up towards the sky, tossing his head back and shouting to the stars, "On a moonless night may my wings take flight, over the valleys and hills I soar, as the ground trembles at my mighty roar!"

The last line he recited was barely understandable, for his voice became guttural and deep, slowly building in volume. He hunched over and fell forward to the ground. His change was rapid and almost instantaneous. His arms grew and stretched like tentacles, his fingers lengthened and a web began growing, connecting them at the tips. His spine bent, contorted, and sprung out in length, each vertebrae popping out grotesquely into long spikes. His hind legs grew and thickened. His tailbone stretched out like a giant spear, forming his tail, tipped with a spaded point. His neck extended and his face cracked and popped as it became the scaly, razor-tooth face of a dragon. His pale skin was now covered in iridescent blue scales, shimmering like the stars themselves, each of his eyes glowing brightly like a fiery blaze against the night sky.

Fully transformed, Azul stood before them, towering mightily and proud. He stretched out his wings, revealing his truly magnificent size and let out a roar with such force that it trembled the earth beneath their feet. He gave a mighty flap of his wings sending out a gust of wind strong enough to bend and shake the trees all around him and stumbled his audience backwards. He stood up on his hind legs, stretching out his neck and flapped his wings once more before sending a tremor through the earth with his weight as he stomped down on the ground in front of him, a plume of dust blowing out from beneath him.

Jule stood in absolute awe, her mouth agape and eyes wide. As much as she didn't like or even get along with Azul, she quickly developed a deep respect of his power. She couldn't believe her own eyes. The giant beast heaved himself into the air with a flap of his wings and took to the skies, disappearing into the darkness.

"This is a rare sight indeed," Loki said to Jule. "According to the dragon legends, only two dragons are present on the earth at a time, one being the European's depiction as Azul is, and one being what the Asian countries depicted. When one dies, it is immediately reincarnated into the next living human born. They are one of the few species blessed with knowing exactly who and what they are from birth. The two dragons that exist act as a yin and yang: one being a fire-breathing dragon, while the other, his opposite, is a female who breathes ice. Azul here is an iridescent blue, I can only assume that the other is red. In all of my lifetimes spent as a mortal on this earth, I have only ever encountered the dragon Azul."

"Do the two dragons ever meet?" Jule asked intrigued by the enchanting stories.

"They say that the two dragons are destined to forever be apart. Their mortal lives lived are so vastly different from one another that they're guaranteed to almost never meet. The pages that went on to describe what could happen if two dragons were to meet were lost a long time ago in history, so no one really knows," Loki said solemnly.

"So, can he only transform on new moons?" Jule asked.

"No, he can do this whenever he wishes. We collectively decided that new moons were the safest time, as he can hide in the darkness and fly unnoticed. The new moon phase happens to be his strongest point of transformation as well, just as you transform easiest on the full moon."

Jule shuddered at the thought of Azul unleashing his arrogance and destroying the town for the sheer fun of it. She recognized his need for power and his insatiable hunger for it. To her, it was only a matter of time before Azul became a real threat and now, with the Order no longer stalking about, she worried that it would happen sooner than later.

"When is he coming back?" she asked, concern rising in her voice.

"He'll be back when he's had his fill of flying for the night, which could take hours. We can go now, if you want to," Loki suggested. "We don't have to wait for him."

Jule nodded in agreement and went back to his truck without a word to anyone. She had a terrible feeling in her gut and yearned to return to William; to be in his arms where she felt safest in the world.

Loki wasted no time and hurried to the truck, sensing Jule's unease. They drove again in complete silence, Jule's mind too distracted with fears and concerns to engage in simple conversation. As they neared William's house, Loki broke the silence.

"So, what did you think? Pretty cool, huh?"

"Oh, yeah, cool I guess." Jule snapped back out of her spinning thoughts. "Can he breathe fire?"

"Yes he can, but since we live in a high-altitude desert and we are in a drought, it's not a good idea. He could set this whole place ablaze and there would be nothing to stop it. That would be devastating."

Jule stirred in her seat.

"What's on your mind?"

"It's just that, well, you know how Azul can be... and now that I see how powerful he really is, what if he becomes a... problem?" Jule raised an eyebrow.

"You think I haven't thought of that or taken that possibility into consideration?" Loki asked, almost offended.

Jule simply shrugged her shoulders and continued staring out the window.

"Well, I have," he replied defensively. "Azul will most certainly be a challenge, if it comes to that, but not impossible. Don't worry about it until that arises, though. No use in fretting over something that hasn't happened yet."

Loki frowned disappointingly.

"It will be such a shame to kill him if it does come to that. Such an incredible and rare beast..." He drifted off with his words.

Loki parked his truck in front of William's house and escorted Jule to the door.

"Are you going to come in?" Jule asked as she paused in the doorway.

"No, I'm going to head back to town, but I'll be back tomorrow. I want to see how far you've come in controlling your transformations."

"Alright." Jule forced a smile. "Drive safe."

They hugged and parted ways, Jule closing the door behind her before heading up the stairs to check on William.

She found him awake and chatting with Rayme about something that made William burst into hysterical laughter, though Jule didn't catch what it was. As she entered the room, they both quieted down and turned their attention to her.

"So, how did it go?" William asked Jule. She sat on the bed next to him.

"It was incredible, honestly, and terrifying at the same time," she admitted.

"He scares you, too, huh?" Rayme asked as he removed his glasses to rub his tired eyes.

"Oh, come on," William chuckled. "That guy is about as scary as a rabid flea."

"I don't know," Jule disagreed. "His fiery-hot temper, instability, and the fact that he can turn into a dragon makes him pretty damn scary to me."

"Look, if he really wanted to lay waste to this town and everyone in it, don't you think he would have done it by now?" William asked.

"Well, consider the fact that he now has a window of opportunity, should he decide to take it," Rayme added.

"What window of opportunity?"

"We know for a fact that the Order of Purity isn't in the area anymore, you took care of that." Rayme gave a wink of approval to Jule. "It will probably be a little while before they send in someone else, so he has a short window where he could wreak havoc as a dragon and take off without the Order hot on his tail."

"That would be a foolish move if he did," William said.

"Indeed, it would," Rayme agreed. "And could you really put it past him to do such an idiotic thing? I mean, the guy isn't exactly a genius, nor does he plan ahead very well or consider consequences. You are aware of the fact that Azul operates mainly on impulse."

Jule and William both nodded.

"It wouldn't be hard for Azul to convince Viktor to partake in his destruction, but what about Demonik?" Jule asked as she was trying to coordinate a plan of defense in her head, needing to get an idea of who all she may have to face.

"Viktor would absolutely join him without a second thought. Demonik, even though he's Azul's brother, he's far more rational. I think if he weighed out the pros and cons of Azul's impulsive idea that he would see how reckless and dangerous it is. I don't worry about him too much. Now, Catarina is another wild, unpredictable individual with a destructive nature, though hers mostly involves devouring someone's soul through sex. I could see her jumping on the band wagon," said Rayme.

William nodded again.

"But she wouldn't be too difficult to deal with; she's the weakest of them," William pointed out.

Jule collected and weighed the information in her head, hashing out a plan.

"So, a dragon, a demon, and a succubus?" she asked.

"Hopefully that's all," said Rayme.

"And what do we have on our side?"

"Well, we have you two, who are, obviously, werewolves. We've got Loki with his cunning, also he has a pretty cool spear, and we've got Athan, who is a wizard, and Fidelia, who is a sneaky little cat nymph."

"Our odds don't sound too great," Jule frowned.

"Eh," William shrugged. "We'll be fine."

His optimism annoyed Jule yet at the same time she found it to be irresistibly cute.

CHAPTER 18

William recovered completely, miraculously returning to his full strength by the next morning. Rayme was highly impressed in the speed of his recovery, remarking on how well his body was able to flush out the remaining silver flecks efficiently.

"I'm so glad you're okay!" Jule exclaimed when Rayme officially cleared him. "I don't know what I would do if I lost you – you're my everything."

William pulled her in and held her.

"I'm not going anywhere," he assured her.

A frantic and panicked knock came from the front door, startling all three of them. Rayme rushed down the stairs to answer as Jule and William crept cautiously out the bedroom, peering down in anticipation.

Rayme opened the door and Loki hurried in with Fidelia, Athan, and Esadora closely behind.

"We have a problem," Loki said, out of breath.

"What is it?" William asked from above.

"The thing we all feared is coming true. Azul is planning something with Viktor."

"Damn, we just can't catch a break can we?" William joked inappropriately.

"How do you know?" asked Rayme.

"I had suspicions after Jule raised her concern about it last night, so I had Esadora perform her spirit immersion on Azul. She embodied him and heard him discussing his plan with Viktor," Loki answered.

Esadora was clearly shaken, still trembling from her experience, fear lingering in her eyes. Jule made her way past William down the stairs to console her, leading her to sit down on the couch. The others followed, gathering as they could in the living room, Fidelia sitting with the girls. William stood behind the couch where they sat. He placed one hand firmly on Jule's shoulder, a gesture to assure her he would protect her.

"What about Catarina?" Rayme asked. "We had some concerns about her as well."

"I don't know, she wasn't there," Esadora responded. "But they're planning on acting tonight, while the new moon is still in effect. Azul plans to destroy the town. He was ranting and raving about how we shouldn't hide anymore and that the people should fear us, so that they will respect us. Viktor was completely on board, extremely eager to cause some destruction himself. He was most excited about *the slaughter.*"

"What do we do?" asked Athan, quietly repeating the question to himself and pacing awkwardly back and forth near the door.

"Yeah, we need a game plan," said Rayme.

"The dragon is going to be the most difficult to deal with, honestly, but we can do it. It'll be extremely advantageous if we can get the jump on him and get him in his human form, but if we can't, we're going to need all the strength we can muster," Loki replied.

"What about the demon? How do you take care of a demon?" Jule asked.

Loki snapped his fingers.

"You get a demonologist to perform a banishment ritual," he replied. "And I know just the one."

"Who?" asked Rayme.

"Jeremy, of course," Loki said.

Rayme and Athan nodded their heads.

"What do we need to do first?" William asked.

"First, I need to find Demonik," Loki replied as he approached Esadora. "I need to know if he is involved or not."

He looked down at her, regretting his request before he even made it.

"Do you think you can do it again for me? Can you immerse into Demonik's entity and locate him?"

Esadora stirred in her seat, her sweet, innocent doe eyes welling up with tears.

"I don't know if I can," she said quietly. "I'm all shook up. I don't think I can concentrate."

"Alright," Loki said with a frown. "I won't make you do anything you don't want to. Stay here with Jule, Fidelia, and William. Take the time you need to calm down."

"She'll be fine here with Jule but I want to come with you if you're planning to go looking for him yourself," William said.

"Are you sure you're up to it?"

"Absolutely." William said with total confidence.

"Athan, Rayme, are you two willing to come with?" Loki asked.

Both gave a silent nod in agreement. The four of them exited the house, leaving the girls behind.

Fidelia and Jule held Esadora together and rocked her as she softly sobbed.

"I'm really scared." She nervously laughed through her tears.

"We'll be okay," Jule lied. She wasn't really sure if they would be okay or not, but she felt the need to say something that would bring her friend some comfort.

"Yeah, we'll be fine." Fidelia said with a confidence that even convinced Jule.

"So, do you know any other beings?" Jule asked Esadora, changing the conversation.

Esadora looked up and wiped the remaining tears from her eyes.

"Yes, a few," she said. "I had this one friend who suffered horribly from depression. One day she decided that she couldn't take it anymore and planned her suicide. She climbed to a high, remote cliff with the intention of jumping. She told me that as she fell to the ground, she immediately regretted her decision and wanted to live. Just before she hit the ground, she said she sprouted these giant white wings from her back and instinctively began flapping them like a mad woman. Her wings prevented her death and lessened the blow of her fall. Instead of dying, she ended up with only a few minor scrapes and bruises. She became a whole new person once she discovered her True Self." Esadora paused and reflected on her friend.

"What was she?" Jule asked. "What do you call that species?"

"A zeraphyn: the biggest influence for the common depiction of angels. She truly became an angel, no longer seeing the negatives of life, but realizing and encouraging the positives," Esadora said, a slight smile spreading across her face.

"That's truly inspiring," Jule said. "What happened to her?"

"I'm not too sure," she replied with a frown. "We fell out of touch years ago when she started traveling the world for charity. I do miss her, though."

The girls continued sharing stories and experiences with Jule about the various other beings they knew and met, which eased their shared worries for the events to come. Jule was amazed at just how many different species existed, and wondered herself who she may meet in the future. The possibilities seemed endless, from shape-shifters to telepaths to elementals. She wondered how many other beings she had already met without realizing it.

"I wanted to ask you," Esadora started. "Are you doing okay?"

Jule looked at her, confused.

"What do you mean?"

"Well, that girl you killed," Esadora began explaining hesitantly. "Wasn't she like, your best friend or something?"

Jule looked down, sadness sweeping over her.

"Yeah, she was," she said softly.

"That must have been really hard for you," Fidelia said as she affectionately rubbed Jule's back.

"It was… it is. We spent so much time together as kids, but as it turns out, everything about her was just a lie."

"How do you mean?" asked Esadora.

"Well, I mean, she was a member of the Order of Purity who was *assigned* to me, to play my friend and get to know me. I feel so robbed. Part of me misses her because of the illusion of friendship she portrayed, but another part of me is glad I killed her, ending the charade. Plus, she was going to kill William. I had to do something! And she tricked Bradley. She was the one who killed him. Well, not her personally I guess, just her bodyguard guys. So, I guess I just have really mixed emotions on the subject," Jule replied and shrugged her shoulders. "No one has really bothered to ask me about it, so thanks," she added with sincere appreciation.

"Damn, that's rough," Fidelia frowned. "I for one am really glad that you got out of there alive *and* saved William. You're one tough bitch." She giggled.

"You're his knight in shining armor!" Esadora joked, sending the girls into a hysterical laughter.

They were interrupted as the front door suddenly opened. All three of them stood up nervously. William led the troop of guys into the house, Demonik, unexpectedly, following them in the rear.

MORE THAN HUMAN

CHAPTER 19

"You're here," Jule said to Demonik in surprise as he entered.

"Yes, yes, I am. You guys need my help."

"You mean you're not siding with your brother?" Jule asked with more skepticism in her voice than she intended.

"No, I am not 'siding' with him. Azul is wrong and Loki is right; it's that simple really."

Demonik bowed his head with apparent sadness.

"We all need to stay hidden," he continued. "The people out there are not ready to know of our existence. Pulling a stunt like Azul is about to do is completely irrational and reckless. He'll draw attention to us, to our home, and to countless other species out there. If he does this, the consequences will be grave and thousands will suffer; both human and non-human alike."

Jule was impressed by his rationality. He was surprisingly level-headed, the polar opposite of his brother.

"So do we have a plan?" asked Fidelia.

"Yes we do," Loki replied.

"Our main goal –" Demonik began explaining, "–is to keep my brother separated from Viktor for as long as we can. I will approach him with the intention of convincing him that I want to take part in his destruction and take him to Loki's bar to talk. While I'm doing that, Loki and William will go to Jeremy's to perform the banishment on Viktor."

"What are the rest of us supposed to do?" Jule asked.

"Anyone else who wishes to help us is welcome, though this will be the most dangerous thing we have done," Loki explained. "Your lives will be in great danger, you may get hurt or even worse – killed. If you don't wish to fight or take part in this, no one will judge you. Stay here. This house is far enough away from town to avoid any destruction should our plan fail and Azul succeed. Also as far as I know, he doesn't know the location of this house, making it even safer for you to hide."

"You and Rayme were the only ones who knew where my house was until a few days ago," William said, sounding somewhat disappointed that more people now knew of his sacred, private place.

"I know, and I am sorry. But, you're willing to let them stay here to remain safe, yes?" Loki asked.

William nodded his head, disapproval written on his face.

"So, with that said, does anyone else want to help?" Loki asked, searching around the room for volunteers.

"I want to stay here," Esadora said ashamed. "I'm not very powerful."

"That's probably best," said Loki, rubbing her shoulder in support.

"I want to help," Jule announced. "I know I'm new to my abilities, but I want to do something."

William placed his arm around her proudly and smiled at her.

"Alright," Loki said. "Athan, what about you?"

"I'll stay here with Esadora, should anything happen here," he replied, predictably repeating his statement quietly to himself. Athan had a very peaceful nature about him. As a natural pacifist, Jule noticed that he would avoid conflicts at all costs. Any time there was discourse among the group, Athan always took the neutral route, refusing to side with anyone on virtually anything. Jule sensed his desire to avoid confronting an angry dragon and empathized with him. Part of her wished she could stay behind.

"Fidelia?"

"I'll help any way that I can," Fidelia replied with a confidence Jule admired.

"Great, we'll figure out what we will need you guys to do." Loki took a short pause. "Rayme will stay here with you two as well and act as the medic," he said to Athan and Esadora. "You two will need to assist him."

"I know where my brother is," Demonik said. "Catarina will most likely be with him. She's been acting strange around him lately, being more secretive and suspicious. I've caught them conspiring together, but they always hushed when I entered the room or something. I have a feeling they've been planning this for some time now. They've just gathered their confidence to act on it now since Jule here took care of the Order problem we had. I know Viktor has been waiting a long time for this."

"Jule, come with me and William. Fidelia, you go with Demonik and play along with his charade to Catarina since she trusts you the most out of us. Convince her that you both want to participate," Loki instructed.

He scanned the room studying his friends' worried and frightened expressions. Immense pride spread across Loki's face as he looked about the room clearly admiring his friends' loyalty. He cleared his throat and addressed them.

"I want you all to know how strong you guys really are. This is no easy feat ahead of us, and it takes so much strength and bravery to be facing it with me. I am proud of all of you and I know Bradley would be proud as well. He's smiling down on us from Valhalla," he paused, closing his eyes and smiling, as if he could feel his deceased brother's bold presence as he spoke.

"No matter what happens –" he continued. "–be proud of yourselves. I know we can do this. May Odin's strength and guidance be with us tonight!"

The group prepared for their various jobs, all giving each other hugs and words of encouragement. William and Jule shared a long, passionate kiss before heading out with Loki, their hands clasped tight.

"Don't touch my stuff!" William shouted over his shoulder as he left.

CHAPTER 20

Jeremy stood waiting on the porch outside of his house when Loki, Jule, and William arrived. Jule didn't get a good look at him as she approached, merely a glance as he quickly turned and led the way into the house. His home was located near the busy downtown, a few blocks uphill from Loki's bar. The streets were crowded with pedestrians and tourists. Jule felt nervous being around so many people, fearing what sort of disaster could befall them at any moment with an angry demon and dragon about. She envied their ignorance of the dangers, wishing that she, herself, wasn't aware of the possible destruction. Her heart pounded, her blood ran hot through her body, tingling everywhere.

William must have sensed her tension and gently held her hand, guiding her through the front door of Jeremy's house. It looked fairly plain on the outside; red brick walls, red shingles, a quaint oak front door, and a few cute floral bushes surrounding a healthy grass yard. This certainly didn't strike Jule as the home of a demonologist, but rather that of a boring librarian. That is, until she stepped inside.

It was dark, hidden behind black-out curtains that hung in every window, allowing in no natural light. Candles that were placed throughout the main room burning on tables and a chandelier were the only source of light. Jule honed in on her wolf vision, allowing her to see more clearly in the darkness of the house. She felt heavy in the room, some sort of energy holding her down like increased gravity pulling at her. A huge red pentagram was painted on the accent wall to her right, from floor to ceiling, decorated with various symbols surrounding it that Jule didn't recognize. She assumed it was Babylonian or maybe Sumerian.

A tall, fair-skinned man with jet black shoulder-length hair parted neatly down the middle approached them in the center of the room. He was unconventionally handsome, Jule thought to herself. He had a very dominant jawline with high cheek bones and dark sullen eyes. A black cloak hung from his body, draping on the floor, the hood resting on the back of his neck. He had long, slender pale hands with black painted fingernails and a remarkably noble presence.

"Greetings," he said as he extended his hand to William.

William shook his hand firmly.

"How do you do?" Jeremy asked as he bowed politely to Jule.

"Uh, hi, nice to meet you," she said, unsure of how to respond to someone bowing before her, being a first for her.

"Welcome to my home, please watch your step and do not disturb anything. Follow me to the back room where I have already prepared the circle and let's get started."

The three followed Jeremy into a small room in the back corner of the house. Jule tightly clasped William's hand nervously. She felt uncomfortable in the house; something was itching inside her to leave, but she forced herself to ignore her feelings and continued into the room.

"Do not step on the circle, please," Jeremy directed. "Don't cross over the perimeter with your hands or feet; don't reach into the circle for any reason."

Jule looked down and at her feet was a five-foot wide pentagram made of salt on the floor. A candlestick was placed at each point of the star and more of the symbols Jule saw from the pentagram on the wall in the living room encircled this one. William, Jule, and Loki carefully positioned themselves around the sacred symbol, careful not to touch it. Jule pushed her back against the wall allowing for as much space between her and the star as possible. Jeremy stood at the head of the star, holding a black bound book with red pages in his hand.

"I will begin the summoning of the demon known as Viktor," he began explaining. "He will appear in the center of the circle and will not be able to cross it. I will have him contained, as long as no one disturbs the perimeter of salt. Once he is trapped, I will then perform a ritual to banish him from this plane. The three of you are here to keep him from escaping, should he cross the barrier for whatever reason. Do not under any circumstances allow him to leave this room until the banishment is complete, otherwise we will lose our only real chance."

Jule nodded her head, her arm outstretched at her side holding William's hand firmly.

"Have you ever done this before?" she asked.

"Yes, well, once. It worked out alright then," Jeremy replied optimistically but not too convincing.

Jule didn't feel very confident in his response and began dreading the worst to occur.

"After you," Loki said gesturing to Jeremy.

The demonologist cleared his throat, his pronounced Adam's apple bobbing up and down as he began reading from his book in some kind of ancient language. Jule couldn't understand the guttural, archaic words that resonated from his mouth, but she feared them. A rumbling began about the room; the floorboards began to quiver beneath their feet, the door rattling as if someone was on the other side frantically trying to get in. Loose papers Jeremy had resting on a table behind him began swirling about like they were caught in a miniature tornado. Jule's hair swirled around her face, strands of hair hitting her eyes. One of the papers floated down near a candle and caught fire. Loki quickly stomped out the embers on the floor, keeping in mind not to touch the circle. Jeremy, unmoved by the commotion, continued his reading without missing a beat. He raised his hands high to the ceiling as he shouted more guttural words, sounding rather evil himself.

Suddenly, a poof of red smoke appeared in the center of the circle. As it cleared, Jule could see Viktor standing in the center, looking rather annoyed and furious. Jeremy ceased his recital from the book.

"How dare you!" Viktor hissed at Loki. "How dare you all!" He glared at everyone, fists balled up at his sides. The candle flame reflected in his eyes as if they were on fire themselves.

"You gave me no choice," Loki said sternly.

"This will never work. I will be back. I will find a way back!" Viktor threatened.

The demon shot a glare at Jule, his eyes burning red with rage. Twisted black horns quickly sprouted from his forehead as he began exposing his true form. His skin changed into a dark red hue, his nails grew out into long black claws. He smiled revealing his sharp, grotesque, and jagged teeth shimmering brightly in the candle light.

Jule's skin crawled with disgust as the creature stared her down, almost peering into her very soul. Her hair stood up on-end. She grimaced as she painfully grew out her own claws, lacking the power of the full moon for a smoother transformation. William protectively stepped in front of her, challenging the demon's fierce gaze. He lengthened his own claws threateningly and pointed one sharp one offensively in the demon's face with a seething grin.

"You're powerless here," William declared. "Jeremy, continue with the banishment."

"No!" Viktor screamed with a roar and pounded his fists against the sides of the invisible enclosure.

He lunged towards William only to be blocked once again by the barrier's invisible force field, knocking him down clumsily onto his back. He furiously shot up and began slamming his fists on the unseen barrier. With each pound of his fists, the barrier zapped with electricity and he howled in frustration again.

Jeremy flipped the pages of his book searching for a specific ritual to perform as Viktor lashed out like a rabid wild animal, desperately trying to free himself of his containment.

"Ah, here it is," Jeremy said with a grin, pointing his index finger down at the printed words.

"Hurry up," Loki said, worried.

"It's too late," Viktor smiled, breathing heavily. "Azul will destroy this town and all of you traitors with it. We will rise up. We will be feared and respected!"

"Not if we can help it," William shot back.

Jeremy picked up a chalice off of the table behind him with his right hand and held his book of rituals in the left, carefully balancing it in his hand and holding it open with his thumb and pinky. He lifted the chalice high into the air above him as he began reading again.

Viktor clasped his clawed hands over his ears, shut his eyes tightly, and fell to his knees on the floor at the sound of Jeremy's voice.

"No, no, no!" he begged.

Jeremy, finished with the first verse of the ritual, turned and placed the chalice back on the table, exchanging it for a brilliant athame with a silver handle tipped with opal. The blade shone in the glimmering candle light as he held it in the air, just as he did with the chalice, and began his chanting again.

Viktor writhed in pain on the ground inside the circle, growling in a foul language with ferocity. Then, he stood up slowly in the center of the pentagram, his head bowed down and his arms relaxed at his sides. The symbols Jule saw painted on the wall and drawn in salt on the floor began to appear on Viktor's skin as if some invisible dagger was carving them in. His entire torso, arms, back, and face became decorated with the symbols, dripping with his fresh, black demon blood. He grinned through the pain as another carved itself into his forehead, wiped away the drip of blood flowing down his face and licked it off his finger, staring hard into Loki's eyes.

Jule shuddered but stood her ground, feeling impatient and wishing for the ritual to end and for the masochistic demon to be banished.

Viktor stomped the ground hard with his foot, forcing a candle on the floor to fall to its side, spilling wax. Jule, worried about a fire spreading, reached down to replace the candle when Loki stopped her.

"No, you'll disturb the circle. Don't touch it," he ordered.

Viktor stared intently at Jule with a low growl and a sinister smirk.

"You!" he snarled. "You have no real friends, no one loves you and you may think you belong here, but you don't!"

"Ignore him," Loki said.

"And you, wolf-boy." Viktor shifted his stare towards William. "You're a weakling. You can't even take care of yourself. Your little girlfriend had to come to your rescue – you're not a real man," he said with a condescending tone.

"He's just trying to get a rise out of you, don't give into it," said Loki. "If you cross the barrier it will break and he will be free."

"Yes, I know your fears, I know your insecurities," Viktor sneered. "Our 'fearless leader' is so afraid that he prevents us from being who we truly are. What concern do you really have for the people of this cursed town? What have they ever done for you? What do you think these people would do if they knew what we really were? Who are you really protecting?"

Loki remained unmoved, silent and firm in his place.

"You're holding yourself back, you know," the demon continued. "You're only still a human because you choose to be. You're afraid of your own potential and you're just jealous of the potential we all have so you try to control us. You're a coward!"

"Shut up!" Loki shouted with his eyes narrowed, slipping and allowing the demon's words to get the better of him momentarily.

Jeremy placed the athame back on the table and lifted a candle into the air and began chanting another verse. Viktor howled with pain as more symbols were carved into his skin. He was almost entirely covered now, bleeding from each new character. Panting heavily he hunched over onto the floor, wrapping his arms around himself. With each word Jeremy recited, Jule saw Viktor's strength diminish more and more.

One final time, Jeremy returned the candle to the table and picked up an eagle feather, holding it up, swirling it around in a circular motion with his wrist, and continuing the ritual. With the last verse being chanted, Viktor's remaining strength left his body and was heaped limply on the floor, breathing heavily and shaking with pain in a pool of his own blood. Jule, for a moment, almost felt sorry for him.

Red smoke began wafting up from the pool of receding blood, encircling Viktor's body in a spiral motion, traveling up inside the barrier to the ceiling. What Jule could only assume was a portal opened in a circle on the ceiling directly above the demon. The smoke continued floating up into the portal, taking Viktor with it. Then the portal suddenly closed, the candles blew out, the commotion ceased and all traces of Viktor were gone. Not a single spot of his blood remained on the floor. The only indication that anything occurred in the room remaining was the knocked over candle which Jeremy carefully picked up and returned to its upright position.

"So he's gone then? Where did he go?" Jule asked as Jeremy turned on the lights.

"You know, I'm not exactly sure where that spell sends them, but I know it works. He's not here anymore, is he?"

"Nope, he's not." Jule said, looking around the room, retracting her claws and allowing herself to relax. "At least I can't see him... but, where did you send him? Is he still on Earth or did you like, send him to some other dimension or something?"

"Like I said, I'm not sure *where* it sends the demons. I just know that it casts them from Earth. Maybe he's chilling on Pluto right now? Who knows?" Jeremy giggled, clearly the only one amused at his joke.

"Are you okay?" William asked Jule quietly.

"Yeah, I'm alright. Just a little shook up. I've never seen a demon before, much less an angry one being banished." Jule laughed nervously.

She held William's hands and looked him in the eyes.

"Is what he said true, though?" she asked him.

"What do you mean?"

"Are you... ashamed that I saved you?" she asked, worried that she had somehow robbed him of his masculinity.

William laughed.

"No," he said. "I'm proud to have you in my life and I am so thankful that you were there. The only thing that I'm ashamed of is the fact that I was caught off-guard in the first place. I should have known better."

He kissed Jule softly on the lips.

"And what he said about you isn't true either," William whispered. "You *are* loved, you *do* belong here. You're my fierce little warrior-goddess." He smirked.

Jule smiled and blushed. As much as she didn't want to admit it, Viktor's words rang true to her. She worried that no one loved her – that she had no friends and that she didn't belong anywhere – but William's words of encouragement subsided her insecurities. She knew he would never lie to her, and she loved him for it.

"Well, that went much better than I was anticipating," Loki said with a sigh of relief. "One down, two more to go. We should go meet up with Demonik and Fidelia back at my bar."

Loki turned to Jeremy.

"Thank you for your help." He shook Jeremy's hand.

CHAPTER 21

As soon as Loki, Jule, and William arrived at the back parking lot of L&B Bar, Jule immediately sensed that something was amiss.

"Be careful guys," Loki warned cautiously as he slowly approached the back door that was unusually left wide open. "Something isn't right."

Jule crept carefully alongside William into the bar. Chairs were strewn across the room inside, tables were flipped over, broken glass spread dangerously across the floor, and the dangling, damaged lights flickered. Jule gasped at the sight of the mess, covering her mouth with her hands in shock.

"What happened here?" she asked aloud.

Loki carefully navigated the destruction, avoiding stepping on anything that would make noise.

"I don't know," he whispered. "But there's a blood trail over here." Loki pointed down to a narrow, but steady trail of blood beginning from behind the bar leading up the stairs to the office above.

Jule and William hurried over to Loki's side to see. The three of them slowly followed the blood trail up the stairs to the closed office door. Loki prepared himself and gently pushed to open it, but was met with some sort of resistance holding the door firmly in place. He pushed on the door harder to no avail. William stepped forward and with a strong heave from both, they freed the door and it opened.

The office was in the same condition as downstairs, everything strewn about in a chaotic mess. William looked down and saw that Demonik's unconscious body was the barricade preventing the door from opening. He quickly knelt down and rolled Demonik onto his back, putting his ear by the vampire's mouth to check for breathing.

"He's alive," he announced to Loki with a sigh of relief.

William noticed blood dripping from Demonik's lips. He leaned down and sniffed it.

"This is Catarina's blood."

Jule gasped.

"Fidelia is over here, behind the desk!" she shouted.

Loki rushed over to assist Jule and lifted Fidelia off of the ground to gently sit her upright resting her back against the wall. Loki spotted a bruise and a small cut on her scalp. Jule gently held Fidelia's chin in her hand, inspecting her friend's closed eyes.

"I think she was just knocked out," Jule said. "I don't see any other injuries on her really."

"Look, here," Loki said, pointing to the corner of the desk. "There's some blood and hair on this."

"Catarina is over here," William said from the closet in the corner. "She's dead."

Loki hurried to the closet, knelt down and checked for her pulse in her wrist. Nothing. He gently laid her limp arm back to her side and rested his hand lovingly on her chest, closing her eyes affectionately with the slender fingers of his other hand.

"There are holes in her neck and her blood on Demonik's mouth," William informed him.

Loki gently turned Catarina's head to the side to inspect her neck. He found two large, gaping holes protruding from her jugular vein. She was bled completely dry, her skin pale and white.

"Looks like Demonik took care of her," he said sadly. "Go see if you can wake him up, will you?"

William obliged, kneeling down and grabbing Demonik by the shoulders, gently shaking him.

"Demonik, wake up," he said.

No response. William shook harder and Demonik gasped awake with his eyes wide, flailing his arms about as if he was fending off an attacker.

"Calm down, it's us!" William said.

Demonik took a moment to snap out of his panicked state and regain his composure.

A loud pounding came from the front door of the bar downstairs.

"Police! Open up!" a voice called out.

Everyone froze in a panic as Loki quickly adjusted his hair and tidied himself, before swiftly running down the stairs to the front door. Jule quietly shuffled to the office doorway and peered through the cracked door down to the bar below, watching in anticipation. He checked for any blood on himself before opening the door to greet the unwanted officers.

"Oh no, the police? What are we going to do? What if they come inside and see the bodies? This is bad!" Jule whispered, her voice shaking as her body trembled in fear.

"Just stay quiet," William ordered. "Trust Loki."

William, Jule, and Demonik listened intently to the conversation downstairs, making sure to keep quiet and not draw any attention to themselves or give the officers any reason to enter the premises.

With a deep breath, Loki slowly opened the door just wide enough to peek his head through, concealing the chaos in the bar. Two male officers in uniform stood before him.

"Can I help you sirs?" Loki asked, keeping his voice and composure as calm as he could.

"We received reports of a disturbance at this location. Are you the owner, sir?" the first officer asked with a pad and pen in hand, ready to write down his notes.

"Yes, I own this bar," Loki said. "What sort of disturbance?"

The officer scribbled something down onto his pad of paper before continuing.

"The report states that there was a lot of yelling and commotion going on. Is everything alright?"

"Oh, that. Yeah, everything is fine," Loki explained. "I couldn't find my wallet and got really frustrated. You know how that goes." He chuckled nervously with a shrug.

The two officers exchanged glances of doubt with each other.

"Mind if we come in and take a look around?" the second officer asked.

Jule's keen eyes caught the tension rising in Loki as his shoulders subtly stiffened beneath his shirt. His breathing quickened and she wondered if the officers also noticed his demeanor. She could hear his heart thumping wildly in his chest. His eyebrows furrowed as he appeared to be deeply contemplating the situation. As if a switch flipped inside of him, Loki's heart rate slowed, his shoulders relaxed, and his confidence returned.

"Sure, come on in," he said with a wave of his hand, backing away from the door and preparing himself.

The officers entered the building and scanned the room, searching for probable cause. They walked around the area slowly, the broken glass on the floor crunching beneath their feet, the blood trail leading up the stairs, the tables and chairs thrown about the place were all successfully unnoticed by them. Whatever Loki was doing was working.

"Is there anyone else here?" the second officer asked.

"No, it's just me here," Loki assured, still deep in concentration.

The officers looked at each other and shrugged their shoulders.

"I don't see anything wrong here," the first officer said to the second as they circled around back to the front door.

"Sorry for the inconvenience," the second officer mumbled. "You have a nice day, sir."

Loki nodded and smiled politely, waving the officers off as they returned to their patrol car parked on the street. He shut the door with a big sigh of relief before returning upstairs.

"What did you do? How did you convince the police to leave?" Jule asked amazed.

"I used an old illusion trick of mine and made them see what I wanted them to see," Loki replied amused at his success.

"Neat trick," William complimented.

"So, tell me what happened," Loki said, turning his attention to Demonik.

"Azul, he knew what we were up to. He saw right through me. I tried to convince him like you asked me to do, but he didn't fall for it. He got angry," Demonik's sentence broke off as he coughed, heaving over in pain clinging to his side. "He tossed Fidelia across the room and we fought. I got him, I know I did. He was bleeding."

"That must have been Azul's blood downstairs," Loki commented. "It looked like it stopped behind the bar. He must have grabbed a towel or something to try and stop the bleeding before taking off."

"Catarina put me into one of her trances and seduced me, distracting me so Azul could escape. It worked," Demonik said with shame. "She became irresistible to me. She told me to feed on her, I think that was the only way she could really keep my attention long enough and she knew it. Loki, I fed on her. I couldn't stop! I killed her. I drank *all* of her blood. Just like last time," Demonik drifted off.

"I'm so sorry," Loki said as he hugged his friend. "I know you loved her."

"I can't do this Loki. I'm sorry; I thought I was strong enough. But I can't go after my brother. You guys are going to have to stop him," Demonik said with his head bowed and began to weep.

"It's okay," Loki assured him. "Can you stand up?"

"Yes, I think so. Azul hit me hard in the ribs and I think he broke a few. They're starting to heal, but man do they hurt," he said as he grimaced, wiping tears from his cheeks.

Loki and William helped Demonik to his feet.

Fidelia began regaining consciousness, groaning and holding her head as she leaned against the wall behind the desk.

"Ugh my head," she said groggily. "What happened?"

"You were thrown against the wall and hit your head on the corner of this desk. You might have a concussion," Jule informed her.

"Oh yeah, I remember now," Fidelia said holding the top of her head. "Azul figured us out."

Jule helped Fidelia stand up. Fidelia rested heavily against the toppled-over desk still visibly dizzy from her injury.

William pulled his cell phone from his pocket and began texting.

"What are you doing?" Jule asked, curious.

"I'm asking for backup. If Demonik is out, we're going to need someone else."

"Who?" Loki asked.

"My friend, Björn," William replied, still texting on his phone. "Okay, he's going to meet us at my house. Let's get Demonik and Fidelia back to Rayme and have them checked out, then we'll go from there?"

"Agreed," Loki answered. "We need to hurry, sunset is quickly approaching. I'll call Rayme and let him know."

Jule helped Fidelia down the stairs as William and Loki assisted Demonik. They piled up in Loki's truck and headed back to the Blood Moon Ranch with no time to lose.

MORE THAN HUMAN

CHAPTER 22

Rayme rushed out of the house as they arrived, ready to carry Fidelia inside. Demonik leaned heavily against Loki as they headed in. William and Jule followed. Rayme gently set Fidelia down on the couch in the living room and rushed to grab his precious bag of remedies. He quickly got to work, creating poultices for both of his patients and brewing a tea that they reluctantly forced down.

"The tea will help ease the pain and make you relax," he persuaded when Fidelia and Demonik hesitated.

A knock at the door startled the group that was already on edge.

"It's okay," William coaxed. "It's a friend." He opened the door and joyfully greeted his guest. An enormous bear of a man with extremely broad shoulders, big hefty chest, and a general large presence about him stepped into the house, William shrinking beside him.

"Hallo," the big man said with a jolly smile and a heavy Swedish accent. "My name is Björn." His light, baby-blue eyes, round cheeks, and blond locks of hair that dangled above his shoulders made this intimidating man seem so kind and gentle at the same time.

"Pleased to meet you and we greatly appreciate your assistance," Loki said as he approached to shake Björn's enormous hand.

"No problem," he simply replied.

"This is Jule," William introduced his new guest to her.

"Very nice to meet you." Björn smiled as he shook her hand gently. His giant grasp completely enveloped hers, making her hand look like that of a child's.

"I'm sorry, but enough with the pleasantries. We are on a time limit, people. Can we figure out what we're doing?" Loki said impatiently.

"Yes, of course," William replied, embarrassed. Björn was one of William's closest friends, and he seemed very eager to introduce his new love. But, now was not the time for that.

"So, what is your ability?" Loki asked Björn. "William has not told me anything about you." He shot a look of disapproval to William for inviting some stranger unacquainted with him.

"I am a were-bear," he said proudly in his exotic accent.

"What's that?" Jule asked, immediately feeling stupid.

"It means that like us turning into wolves, he can transform himself into a bear. And unlike us, who rely on the power from the moon, he relies on no celestial power, therefore he can transform at will at any time and with great ease," William explained.

"Oh," Jule said quietly to herself, feeling foolish for asking such a question.

"I take it you're strong?" Loki asked as he closely examined the newcomer.

"Eh, pretty strong," Björn replied with a smile and a shrug of his behemoth shoulders.

"You know we have to take on a dragon?" Loki asked, now skeptical in William's decision to call this guy and only this guy, disregarding the physical appearance of the choice.

"Yes, Will tolds me everything. So whens do we start?" Björn clasped his hands together and rubbed them together excitedly as he smiled.

Jule was impressed at the newcomer's enthusiasm.

"Well, first we need an idea of where Azul is," Loki said, turning to Esadora. "Hopefully he isn't already at the clearing."

Esadora shifted uncomfortably in her seat.

"Please," Loki begged. "We need you to do this."

Esadora reluctantly complied.

"I can't do it here. I need to go into the other room where there aren't any distractions. Loki, you come with me," she said, getting up. "Jule, can you come with me, too?" Esadora's voice broke as she made the request.

"Of course." Jule obliged.

Jule wrapped her arm around Esadora's neck as they followed Loki into the other room for privacy. Esadora sat on the floor while Loki closed the door, promptly locking it, and Jule sat on the edge of a small recliner in the corner. Esadora situated herself by crossing her legs in front of her, placing her hands on her knees, breathing deeply and slowly, beginning her immersion.

Loki watched her intently with anticipation. His right leg bounced up and down impatiently, rocking the bed he was sitting on. Jule shot him a stern glance and mouthed the words "chill out".

"Can you tell us what's happening? What do you see?" Loki pressed.

Esadora took a deep breath.

"I'm trying to hone in on Azul's location," she said, her voice barely a whisper. "There he is."

Her physical form relaxed limply as her spirit left, leaving her pale and lifeless once again.

"He's angry," the corpse spoke. "He's anxious," it continued. "He's concerned about the time. He's running out of time."

"I can't wait for Viktor any longer," a strange, deep voice growled from the corpse. Jule jumped at the sudden change. *That wasn't* her *voice*.

"He has to go now," Esadora's voice returned.

Suddenly Esadora's spirit snapped back into her own body with a jolt. Her head jerked back and she gasped loudly as it happened. Loki rushed to her side, preventing her from falling over from exhaustion. She lay back in his arms trembling and panting.

"He's at his house but he's leaving," she said through heavy breaths. "He was waiting for Viktor, but he got impatient and left. You guys need to hurry."

"Thank you," Loki said as he gently kissed her forehead and helped her to her feet.

They returned downstairs with the news.

"If we leave now we can beat Azul to the clearing. Let's go," Loki instructed.

Jule, William, and Björn wasted no time rushing outside.

"We'll take my truck," Loki announced as he jumped in and started it up.

Jule and William crammed together into the back seats of the truck as Björn, the biggest of the bunch, took the front passenger seat.

Loki sped off towards the clearing, his truck sliding and fish-tailing around each corner, making Jule very nervous.

It won't do us any good if we don't get there alive, she thought as Loki swerved around another corner. She clung tight to William, preparing herself for them to crash.

Miraculously, Loki made it to the clearing without even a scratch on the truck. Jule was impressed at his radical yet extremely precise driving skills.

Loki parked the truck in a hidden area behind a grove of oak and his passengers quickly exited the vehicle. He reached inside of his truck and lifted a large silver rod from its mount above the back window.

"What's that?" Jule asked. She noticed him holding the mysterious object in his hand.

"This is my spear," Loki replied. "It was a gift given to me a very long time ago when I spent some time in Ireland. It is called Lugh."

His thumb found a button near the base of the rod and pressed it. The rod mechanically shot out extending another four feet and revealing a beautiful, shiny blue spaded tip. He stood proudly with it by his side.

"The odds are in our favor right now, but that can quickly change. We need to be ready for when Azul arrives. Taking him by surprise will be our best chance so I need you three to go transform and wait inside the tree line to ambush him," Loki ordered. "Try to stay downwind. If he transforms, attack his wings to keep him grounded where he's most vulnerable. I will do my best to reason with him before we resort to an ambush, but don't count on it working. And I'd rather not kill him unless we are left with absolutely no other choice." Loki requested.

Jule fought her fear and followed William across the clearing to the trees, making sure that they were downwind from where they expected the dragon would appear. Björn trotted off a few yards away from them, seeking his own private area to conduct his change. They all removed their clothes, neatly piling them in a convenient spot, and began their transformations.

Björn achieved his full transformation in just a few short seconds, ambling heavily out of the bushes as he finished. Jule and William, on the other hand, took a little bit longer, relying on the power within themselves rather than the energy of the full moon to ease their transition. Fully transformed, the two wolves stood side-by-side for the first time. William noticed Jule's enormous size compared to his own, humbling him down a bit. Jule realized how much larger she was than her partner, standing a full head above him. She found it oddly ironic how much taller he was than her in his human form, yet how massive she was next to him in her wolf form. They sniffed each other with tails wagging, unable to resist their natural animal instincts.

The wolves' eyes gleamed in the darkness, reflecting the minutest amount of light, shimmering like the flames of candles in the night.

"Now that we are both in this form, we can communicate to one another," William's voice telepathically spoke to Jule's mind.

Her eyes widened as she cocked her head to the side with interest.

"That's awesome," she replied without a word from her lips. *"What do we do now?"*

"We wait for Azul," he said, crouching down.

The great Kodiak bear ambled up to them causing the ground around them to shake, his huge jowls dripping with saliva. The bear's immense size dwarfed Jule. William's back barely reached the bear's ribs whereas Jule stood even with his shoulders. The three beasts hunkered down in the bushes and waited, their muscles quivering impatiently with anticipation.

A great-horned owl hooted from a nearby tree, breaking the eerie silence. Jule's ears twitched to listen intently to every sound, from the wind whistling through the pine needles of the conifers to the distant rumbling of an approaching thunderstorm. The breeze drifted over her fur, tickling her body. She shook and shifted her weight in her crouched position, her claws anxiously digging into the cool, damp dirt beneath her paws.

A few moments later, the distant sound of an approaching vehicle traveling down the dirt road alerted the beasts. Their eyes locked on to the headlights as they peeked in and out of the pine and juniper trees, a large dust trail lit up by the red tail lights following.

The truck came to a stop at the edge of the clearing and Azul stepped out. He wearily looked around with clear signs of suspicion.

"I know you're here, Loki!" he called out into the night. "I know you want to stop me, but that's not going to happen."

"Great, he knows we're waiting for him," Jule said to William telepathically.

"No," he replied. *"He knows Loki is here. We are the surprise. As long as we remain downwind from him, he won't be able to sniff us out. This is an ambush, remember?"*

Azul slammed the door of the truck as Loki stepped out clearly into view.

"I knew it," Azul said with a smirk. "So, what? Do you have some long, boring, mundane speech you want to deliver? Because you can save your breath. All you ever do is talk. Talk and give orders. Well, I'm tired of taking your orders. I'm tired of being controlled by you!" Azul stopped and stood firmly in place, his shoulders rigid with anger.

"I've come to reason with you, if that's possible," Loki calmly explained.

Azul glared in the darkness silently.

"Azul, don't do this," Loki began to plead. "This isn't right, brother."

"How dare you call me 'brother'!?" Azul snarled back with insult through his teeth. "I am no *brother* to you! You let your brother die. You're just a coward. You're afraid to let any of us be who we really are. You're jealous of the rest of us because we have power whereas you do not. Your so-called power was denied by the gods. You're a pathetic human living out his fantasy vicariously through us. All you want to do is control us. Well, not anymore! I will not hide! I will not be a coward like you! We should be *feared*. We should be *worshiped* by these pathetic humans, not hunted down and exterminated like vermin hiding in the shadows."

"I hide us to protect us. Not because I'm afraid of the humans, but because they can't handle our existence. This will bring on so much more devastation than you can imagine, but you're so blinded by your own ego that you refuse to see anything at all. Your actions are calling for war!"

Loki reached his arm back and removed his spear from behind him, allowing Azul to see his weapon and giving a silent warning as he pressed the button that extended it. A glint of hesitation, recognition, and fear quickly shot over Azul's eyes as Lugh gleamed with its magnificent blue hue. He knew exactly what that weapon was.

Azul quickly fled towards the field, rapidly preparing his change in desperation.

"I'm telling you now, Azul. Stop," Loki warned with a strict parental tone as he calmly followed.

Azul's eyes glowed orange as he shot back a toothy sneer and began to transform. Jule searched her companions for a sign to move in, but neither budged. Her eyes fixed back on Azul and she watched in anticipation.

Loki suddenly pounded the end of the spear into the ground with such force that a shock wave burst out, shaking the trees all around and causing Azul to stumble onto his side mid-transformation, interrupting the process. The half-dragon, half-man swung his awkwardly elongated neck around only to find that Loki had vanished.

"Tricky, tricky." The grumbled words were distorted as Azul's human face continued to morph into the dragon's, his jaw changing shape and his lips receding into scales. He stood back up, swinging his head about from left to right as he searched for Loki. An intense bright blue flash of light appeared, encircling the dragon, blinding it for a moment. Azul grimaced, closing his eyes tightly and rubbing them instinctively with his scaly wrists. He peered up and was faced with over a dozen Loki's standing around him, all armed with the blue spear in hand. A sudden look of surprise took over the dragon's face. He viciously snapped and snarled, angrily spewing flames all around him like an uncontrollable fire hose, desperately trying to hit his target. As the flames threatened to burn Loki, he vanished and reappeared instantly, narrowly missing the fire each time.

All at once, each Loki drew back his arm and hurled the spear at the dragon. In an instant, the copies of Loki dissolved into the air and the real Loki stood alone in front of the dragon, his spear piercing the shoulder of the great beast.

Azul threw his head back and howled in pain. Furiously, he locked his eyes on Loki and prepared to spew his fire. Loki stood ready and as soon as the dragon let loose his fiery rage, he vanished once again. With another flash of blinding blue light, a dozen copies of Loki reappeared surrounding the dragon. The spear vanished from the dragon's shoulder leaving a gaping hole with blood pouring out of it and returned to all of the copies' hands.

Throwing his head back he fiercely roared into the night, a tornado of angry fire spewing from his mouth. A crack of lightning and a rumble of thunder echoed over the valley. The dry grass in the field ignited from the dragon's dripping flames and the fire spread rapidly, engulfing the area in which Loki danced around the dragon in a cocky display of wit.

Azul realized that his opponent was much too quick for him. In a desperate attempt to outsmart the god, Azul spread his wings and began to take flight.

"Now!" William's voice shouted in Jule's head as he sprang forward to attack.

"Go for the wings!" Loki shouted.

The great bear roared as he tore off from the tree line towards Azul. William quickly followed and without hesitation. Jule galloped towards the scaled beast. Her fur singed as she leapt over the ring of fire.

The bear, less agile than the wolves, attacked the underbelly of the beast, clawing furiously in an attempt to break through the tough reptilian hide, pulling the dragon back down to the ground. William pounced onto Azul's back, grabbing the base of the dragon's long neck with his powerful jaws. Azul let out a thunderous cry in pain.

The dragon flapped his wings violently trying to get away. Jule jumped into the air and grabbed a hold of his wing in her mouth, tearing a hole in the webbing. She lost her grip and crashed onto the ground, her mouth filled with flesh and thick blood. She spat it out and struck again, attacking the dragon's vulnerable and exposed throat. Her body swung back and forth as her jaws kept hold.

The beasts violently struggled in a fury of fur and scales. Azul managed to grab William in his mouth and tossed the wolf to the side like a rag doll. The dragon kicked his hind leg forward, releasing Björn's hold on his stomach. The bear flew back and rolled through the fire, his side gashed by a claw. Weakly, he stumbled away from the flames and rolled in the grass, extinguishing himself before collapsing onto the ground. With a mighty heave, the dragon swung himself to the side, launching Jule away from him as she narrowly missed landing directly in the fire. She sprang to her feet, panting heavily and wincing as her ribs throbbed in pain.

With Azul's head turned and his attention fixated angrily on the beasts, Loki saw a window of opportunity. Without hesitation, he threw his spear and struck the dragon square in the chest. Azul howled in pain, fear illuminating his eyes. Another crash of lightning rumbled over the valley as the rain began to fall. The flames hissed and spat in protest as they were slowly extinguished.

"I don't want to do this, Azul," Loki begged for the final time. "Please don't make me."

The dragon breathed heavily as he weakly reached his jaws down and pulled the spear out, letting Lugh drop to the ground before him. Jule caught his gaze for a moment as the dragon seemed to sadly look around, his blood pooling beneath him. Azul flapped his wings as hard as he could muster in a last effort to flee. Jule lunged up at the dragon in an attempt to hold him down, but he had gained too much distance and she fell in vain. Loki picked up his spear and thrust it one last time, striking the beast in the neck. Azul roared painfully as he continued flying off into the distance, struggling to stay air-born with each beat of his tattered wings. With a snap of Loki's fingers the spear appeared back in his hand, dripping with blood.

Jule sprinted towards William who had finally regained just enough strength to stand.

"I'm fine," he said to her. *"Go check on Björn."*

She found the bear unconscious in the damp grass, smoke still rising from his singed fur. She paused, looking for signs of life. The great bear let out a pained, labored breath. Relieved, she instinctively sniffed at his wound and gently lapped up the blood, whimpering quietly. Loki approached and knelt down beside Björn, inspecting his injury.

"Don't worry about him," Loki said reassuringly. "He's a big guy, his wounds will heal, in time."

Loki stood up and removed his phone from his pocket, carefully shielding it from the rain under his cloaked hood.

"Rayme, I need you to get the big bed ready. We have an injury," he directed before hanging up.

William transformed back to his human self and gathered the hidden clothes. Jule collected her own clothes in her mouth and limply wandered off to find privacy to change. Still shaking from the intense rush of adrenaline, it was difficult for her to will herself to change back to her human form. With every attempt she made, her wounded body protested with shocks of pain. She took a deep breath and focused intently on her human form. Slowly, yet painfully, her fur began to recede as more and more of her human characteristics took their rightful place. Finally transformed, she cautiously stood up to get dressed, her legs trembling weakly beneath her. As she straightened her body to stand, her world suddenly went black and she collapsed unconscious in the dark.

MORE THAN HUMAN

CHAPTER 23

Jule lifted her head up from William's lap in the back of the moving truck and looked out the window to get a sense of where they were. Her eyes struggled to focus. In the darkness, she didn't recognize the area, only that they were still somewhere in the wilderness. She noticed the unmistakable halogen headlights of Rayme's car following a short distance behind them out the back window. She turned to William who had fallen asleep with his head bouncing against the side of the window, his wounds already healing.

Jule shifted her position in her seat and stared exhausted out the windshield. As they peaked a hill in the road, an ominous orange glow began to appear. The glow grew before them and rose into a hellish fire spread across the road, blocking their way. Loki slammed the brakes and halted the truck with Rayme skidding to a stop in the dirt behind them. The sudden jolt woke William with a start.

"What's going on?" he asked. "What the hell is this?"

"I don't know," Loki responded putting the truck into park. "I'm going to go check it out."

William followed Loki to investigate and Rayme trotted up to join. Jule sat in her seat, her heart pounding with fear and confusion. *Where did this fire come from,* she asked herself.

The earth suddenly began to tremble as something huge started climbing the cliff face below the road. Jule looked out the window and peered down. A dragon's face came into view, its huge wings expanded outward as it reached the road, its iridescent scales glowing and shimmering in the light of the flames as he crawled up the cliff like a demon crawling out of the pit of Hell.

"No! What the fuck!?" Jule screamed.

Loki, Rayme, and William looked upon Azul in disbelief. The dragon reared his head back and spewed out a fiery plume, engulfing the three unsuspecting victims in flames and disintegrating them. Jule looked on in horror, her eyes flowing with tears, her body frozen in fear. The glowing eyes of the beast locked on to hers and narrowed with an evil glare. He took in a deep breath and spit his fire onto the truck. Jule screamed in terror as the hot flames burst the windows into bits and melted the interior like wax.

"Wake up!" William's voice shouted as he shook Jule's shoulders. "You're having a nightmare."

Jule opened her eyes and found herself lying on William's bed in his room. Unable to control the emotions brought on by her terrible dream, she curled up into a ball and began sobbing heavily into a pillow.

"Hey, hey, it's okay," William said softly. "You're here with me, you're safe." William gathered Jule up in her little ball and cradled her in his arms, gently stroking her hair and kissing her cheek. His affections soothed Jule and her tears stopped. She looked up at him and kissed him on the lips.

"Thank you," she said quietly.

"For what?" William chuckled.

"For being here with me."

William held her tightly in his arms and smiled.

"I'll always be here for you," he replied. "How are you feeling? Can you get up?"

Jule struggled to sit herself upright, her ribs still tender from impacting the ground. She grimaced as she scooted herself to the edge of the bed.

"Let me help you." William rushed to her side and held out his hands to assist her in standing.

Carefully, they made their way down the stairs to the living room where William sat Jule down on a couch.

"Are you hungry?" he asked, heading to the kitchen.

"Not really," Jule muttered. "Can I just have some coffee?"

"Sure," William smiled and obliged to her request.

"How long was I out?" Jule asked as she stretched her tired limbs out in front of her with a big yawn.

"About two days," he answered. "That was a lot for your body to go through, I can only imagine how you feel. Those things don't bother me anymore; now it's just my age that aches my joints. I heal pretty quickly, but I'm getting old," he laughed.

"Shut up," Jule chuckled. "You're not old."

William's cell phone rang from his pocket.

"Hey, Loki," he answered.

Jule got up from her seat and politely made her way onto the back porch, giving William's conversation some privacy.

She breathed in the damp, cool air as she cupped her coffee in her hands and leaned against the railing. The early setting sun sinking slowly below the hills brought a sudden shift in the wind and a drop in temperature. She felt a sense of relief and for the first time in a long time, a true moment of peace. She was undeniably happy and proud of herself. She was fierce and strong – she felt her true sense of belonging. She was *home*.

She recognized the mighty raven King soaring about over the field in front of her, the sun dancing on his back. He shifted his direction in the wind and began flying towards the porch, something shiny dangling out of his beak, glistening in the light. He soared effortlessly towards her, surprising her as he perched on the railing beside her. King extended his neck out towards her, offering her the gift he carried in his mouth. Jule held out her hand shakily beneath his beak as he dropped the object that heavily landed in her palm. She picked up the gift and studied it, seeing that it was a sterling silver Nordic bracelet with a wolf howling at the moon in the center of it. King gave a low, guttural coo more than a caw as he bowed his head down before her. Jule rubbed her finger down the top of his head to his neck, fluffing up his feathers. King gently closed his eyes and stepped closer to her.

With her right hand, Jule clasped her beautiful gift onto her left wrist. The bracelet sat upon her small, delicate wrist so perfectly it was as if it had been crafted just for her. She looked down at the silver jewelry, admiring the detail glistening in the orange glow of the sunset. *A sign from the Universe,* she wondered to herself, *a gift from a mysterious God or Goddess?* She considered the possibilities and chuckled to herself at the ridiculous idea that a deity would reach out to her – plain old Jule. Regardless, she adored her new bracelet and thanked King for his generous gift with a smile and polite, low bow.

The door suddenly opened behind her, startling King as he took off from the railing. William joined her by her side, gazing out lazily over the field of grass dancing to and fro hypnotically in the breeze. Jule reached her arm around his waist and pulled him closer, resting her head on his chest.

"What's that?" he asked, noticing the bracelet.

"It's a gift from King," she said, holding her wrist up to give him a better view.

"What?" William exclaimed. "All he ever brings me are things like bottle caps, pieces of tin, hair ties, you know… trash." He laughed. "That's really cool, though. He must really like you."

"So, what did Loki have to say?"

"Oh, he is coming over in a little bit with Esadora. Is that okay?"

"Why are you asking me? This is your house."

William chuckled nervously.

"Well," he said as he pulled Jule's chin up to meet her eyes, "I was kind of hoping that this would be your home, too."

"Wait, what are you asking?" Jule's voice quivered with excitement, her eyes lighting up.

"I want you to live here with me," he said, his voice soft as silk. "I can't even begin to imagine my life without you in it. You are my whole world. Be with me," he pleaded softly.

Jule's stomach fluttered.

"Of course I will," she said giddily. "I love you, William."

"I love you, too, Jule." William smiled. He leaned down and kissed her, swinging her gently back and forth in his arms.

"You have given me so much," Jule said quietly as their lips parted. "You've given me a place where I truly feel at home, you've given me so much support and you've helped me become who I was meant to be. I don't know how I could ever repay you for that."

"Being part of your happiness is a reward in itself." He grinned. "I would do anything for you."

"I don't know what I did to deserve this – to deserve you, but I'm glad this is happening."

Jule squeezed William tightly in her arms.

"Ow!" she grimaced, then laughed. "My ribs are still sensitive, I guess."

William chuckled as he lessened his grip around her and gently kissed her cheek.

"Sorry," he whispered in her ear.

"Is Björn still here?"

"No, he was healed enough to go home yesterday. We've got the house to ourselves."

Jule stepped back from William and turned her gaze towards the sunset. Enormous fluffy thunderheads building on the horizon glowed with brilliant oranges and pinks, slowly fading into a darker red before losing their life into the darkness, occasionally illuminated by flashes of lightning.

Loki arrived with Esadora about an hour later. The summer thunderstorm had settled in and was pouring down rain. Jule greeted Esadora with a gentle hug, minding her sore body.

"How are you feeling?" Loki asked Jule as he entered the house.

"Still a bit sore, but getting there," she said. "So, what brings you guys here?"

"The other night, while we were occupied with Azul, apparently Demonik disappeared," Loki explained. "Esadora was unable to locate him."

"We were all sitting around talking about, you know, whatever, when he stood up without a word and went out the door," Esadora said with a shrug. "Athan followed him outside but it was like he just *vanished*. I can't lock on to him either."

"Is this going to be a problem?" William asked Loki.

"I don't believe so," Loki replied. "Rayme called me early this morning to tell me that Demonik was there and that he took Catarina's body and left. That was the last time he was seen. Perhaps he's going to bury her himself. You have to remember what he went through, too. He once again killed someone he loved through feeding and his brother betrayed us all. Demonik has been through a lot. Maybe he left to go find himself."

"Or, maybe he left to go find his brother," William chimed in with concern.

"That's just a possibility that we will have to keep in mind," Loki said. "But what can we do about it right now? Until we have a way to locate them…" He shrugged.

Esadora dropped her eyes in disappointment.

"It's not your fault," Loki said reassuringly as he placed his hand gently on her shoulder.

"Can you not immerse with anyone or is it just Demonik?" Jule asked.

"It's just Demonik. I don't understand it. It's like he doesn't even exist," Esadora said with frustration.

"Do you think… he's dead?" William asked Loki.

"Something tells me that he isn't," Loki said as he stood up and began pacing the room. "He has chosen to hide himself, very well, I might add. He's still out there. I'm sure that in time, when he is ready, he will reveal himself again."

Loki paused for a moment by the window before continuing.

"William, I would like to ask for your permission to perform a funeral rite on your private lake."

The sudden change in topic took everyone by surprise.

"Yes, absolutely," William said without hesitation.

"Tomorrow at dusk we will bid my brother a final farewell," Loki said quietly. "Rayme has preserved his body with oils and cloth. I have some ceremonial supplies that need to be prepared. I will need your assistance in the morning, William, to gather it all and set everything up."

William nodded solemnly.

"Oh, and you'll need to provide a burial offering as well," Loki added.

"Jule, when are you heading back home?" Esadora asked, flipping the subject.

Jule and William looked at each other and smiled.

"I *am* home," she said happily. "I'm staying here, with William."

"That's great!" Esadora cheered with excitement. "We can hang out all the time, now!"

"There's always a position for you to work at my bar," Loki offered.

He turned to William.

"And I'll need a hand in running it," he added.

"Sure, anything you need," William said holding out his hand to shake Loki's.

"Fantastic," Loki said pleased. "Well, thank you for the visit, but I think we need to get going." Esadora rose from her seat and followed him to the door.

"Until tomorrow," he gave a farewell.

Alone together once again, William turned to Jule and grabbed her, pulling her close and kissed her. Jule giggled and wrapped her arms around his neck.

"What do you want to do now?" William asked between kisses.

"I dunno, what did you have in mind?" Jule whispered back.

"Are you feeling up for a run on all fours?" he smirked. "It's a beautiful night out and the storm has passed."

"I think I could muster a transformation," Jule said with a smile.

William grabbed her hand and ran out the back door to the field. They aggressively took each other's clothes off by the fire pit and changed into their wolf forms, Jule doing her best to ignore the additional pain from her recovering injuries. William nipped at Jule playfully with his teeth before tearing off across the field, daring her to chase him. She quickly followed in pursuit, catching his tail in her jaws before passing him and leading the way. They engaged in a teasing game of cat-and-mouse, testing their agility, strength, and speed late into the night.

MORE THAN HUMAN

CHAPTER 24

The golden morning sun crested the hill and fell gently upon the resting wolves, stirring them awake from their peaceful slumber nestled together in pine needles. Jule stretched out her legs in front of her, arching her back and yawning wide. She rose her snout and sniffed the early morning breeze, breathing in deeply the damp, sweet air. William stood up and shook his whole body, sending the dew that had collected on his fur overnight misting into the air. They trotted groggily side by side and returned to the house, washing up, and preparing themselves for the day.

Jule found her backpack lying on the floor at the foot of the bed. She rummaged through it, her hand hitting something metal and familiar. She remembered Loki's request for an offering and pulled her Celtic dagger out of the bag.

"This will be perfect to offer for Bradley," she said to herself as she took a moment to admire the craftsmanship, the balance of the blade, and the large ruby that tipped the handle. Her favorite dagger out of her humble collection of knives. It went with her anywhere she traveled and she reflected on how fitting it would be to send it on its final destination with her dear friend. She fastened the dagger over her belt with the loop in the black leather hilt and headed downstairs to make some coffee.

A vehicle honked from outside, interrupting William and Jule's mid-coffee conversation. William stood up from the kitchen table and opened the front door to greet the arrived guests. Jule sipped her coffee as

Loki and Esadora entered the kitchen, grief in their eyes. She set her coffee down, standing up to hug Esadora and offer her a seat at the table. She then turned and hugged Loki before returning to her chair.

"Do you guys want any coffee?" William offered.

"No, thanks. We should really get started if we're going to perform the funeral rite. There's a lot to do. Rayme will arrive transporting my brother's body with Athan this afternoon. We don't have long to prepare."

"Alright," William complied. "We'll see you girls later, then." He kissed Jule lovingly on the forehead before departing out the door with Loki.

"So, is it serious with you and William?" Esadora inquired.

"You know," Jule sighed gleefully. "I really feel like he is my soul mate, though I don't really believe in soul mates. Then again, just a few weeks ago, I never believed that any of this was real, either." Jule gestured generally around her with her hands and chuckled.

"Well, I'm happy for you." Esadora smiled and placed her hand on Jule's knee. Her hand lingered for a moment before she caught herself and quickly pulled away. "There's something I've been wanting to talk to you about," she admitted sheepishly.

"What?" Jule asked, her curiosity piqued, taking subtle note of Esadora's strange lingering contact with her hand.

"I've been noticing that after I do an immersion," she began, "that a little bit of that person's personality remains in me."

"What do you mean?" Jule pressed.

"Well, like Azul, for example. I feel his anger burning deep inside me, in a way. I'm not an angry person at all, you know that, but I've noticed that I've been having more bursts of anger and frustration. Ever since I immersed with him," she explained.

"That's really interesting," Jule replied. "Are you sure it's not just hormones or something?"

"No," Esadora said quietly. "There's more than just the anger. I'm experiencing feelings that really aren't my own."

"Like what?" Jule pressed again.

"Well, this is really embarrassing to admit, but ever since I immersed with William, I've felt an inexplicable attraction to you that I've never had before. A deep yearning and a passionate love."

Esadora paused a moment, her cheeks flushed bright red. She looked as if she felt foolish for confessing to Jule. Jule remained silent, her words escaping her, shifting in her seat unsure how to handle this or how to make her friend feel better.

"But, these aren't *my* feelings," she continued. "I like you, but not like that. We're friends!" She chuckled nervously as she tried her best to not offend Jule in any way.

Jule's own feelings of attraction towards Esadora began to surface. She momentarily fantasized about sharing both Esadora and William in a lover's triangle. A sudden wave of guilt came over her for having such thoughts and she quickly suppressed them once again by reminding herself that those feelings weren't truly shared and that she had already silently pledged her loyalty to William. She felt embarrassed for having such impure thoughts about her friend and mentally punished herself.

"I don't want this to be weird, but I wanted to be honest with you," Esadora said.

"It's okay, I won't take it personally," Jule finally managed to say.

"He really loves you, you know…" Esadora added. "I've never felt anything like that before. He has such a strong, passionate feeling towards you. I never thought anyone could feel that strongly for someone else. You're lucky. I wish I had that."

Jule's heart fluttered rapidly. She felt the same way about William, but she also felt that she wasn't worthy of his love, that she wasn't good enough for him. Conflicting emotions began to arise as her low self-esteem started to kick in.

"I'm sorry you're going through this. That's got to be frustrating to feel things that aren't *you*. Did you tell Loki?" Jule wanted to change the subject.

"Yes, he says that it should pass in time; that these lingering personalities will eventually fade."

"Well, that's good," Jule said. "Maybe it would be a good idea to limit yourself on how often you perform your immersions, just until you get a better handle on it?"

"That's a good idea." Esadora forced a smile. An awkward and uncomfortable silence set in.

Jule pondered at the feeling of sharing emotions with that of another as she sipped her coffee and stared silently out the window. Esadora fidgeted in her seat.

"Do you want to watch some TV or something?" Jule offered.

"Yeah, sure," Esadora agreed. The girls got up and made their way into the living room, switching on whatever grabbed their interest to distract their troubled thoughts.

A few hours later, Loki and William returned sweaty, covered in dirt and sticky tree sap from their labor.

"We've got quite a load of wood out there in the truck. When we get to the spot, I'll need everyone's help unloading," Loki announced as he washed his hands in the kitchen sink.

"Rayme should be arriving soon, right?" William asked.

"He and everyone else attending will meet us at the lake. I gave them all directions," Loki explained. "We should all get going out there soon. We only have a few hours until dusk."

The group crammed themselves into Loki's crowded truck and headed down a narrow dirt road that trailed off behind William's house, winding up and down between the trees. Loki wandered too close at times to trees and shrubs that hugged the tight road, scraping the paint of the truck against the stiff branches as he navigated the trail. Jule's body cringed at the high-pitched noise that shrieked like nails on a chalkboard.

Within an hour, the troop arrived at their destination. The dirt road dead-ended into a small parking area a few yards from the bank of the lake. Loki and William began unloading the piles of wood they collected and neatly piled them into a square pyre near the bank.

"There are a few bags of bundles of herbs in the back of the truck there," Loki said to the girls. "Can you guys get them out and set them over here please?"

Esadora and Jule gathered up the eight cloth bags crammed full of aromatic plant clippings and placed them where Loki directed. Jule picked through the herbs curious to know what he had harvested. She recognized the stiff, woody branches of rosemary topped with quaint bluish-purple buds, long delicate wands of purple blooming lavender, lush bundles of wild mint, and branches of grayish sage.

Loki returned to the truck and pulled out a large, heavy object protected and concealed in a dark blue cloth with white runic lettering stitched along the edges. He cradled it delicately in his arms as he carried it to the base of a towering black pine tree that had an old lightning scar running down the length of the trunk. With great care, Loki leaned the mysterious object against the bottom of the trunk where the lightning scar disappeared into the earth. Jule wondered if this tree in particular held some sort of special significance, but chose to remain silent as she respectfully observed and awaited further instruction.

Loki went back to his truck once again, this time returning with a sizable steel hammer decorated with carvings of Celtic knots around the sides of the head, a hand-carved dark oak handle that burned with runic symbols stuck out from the middle, two leather tassels tipped with silver beads dangled at the end. He placed the heavy hammer on the ground next to a large flat rock that seemed to have been placed intentionally between the pyre and the tree.

A loud rumbling engine noise approached as an old, beat up van came down the road. Rayme carefully maneuvered the van and parked it backwards, positioning the rear to face the completed pyre. Athan, Fidelia, and Jeremy climbed out one by one of the front passenger door and they all gave a quick greeting to one another. Loki opened the rear doors of the van. Inside, Bradley's body rested covered in a heavy cloth on a gurney. Jule's heart sank as she looked upon the concealed body.

William, Rayme, and Athan all assisted Loki in removing Bradley's body and positioned the gurney near the pyre.

"We'll need to have the fire burning for at least two hours before placing Bradley on the pyre. The fire needs time to adequately heat up in order to cremate his body," Loki explained. "For those of you who are unfamiliar with how Nordic funerals go, I will explain."

Loki took a seat in the dirt near the bank of the lake and gestured for everyone else to do the same. He gazed out over the lapping water at the shore's edge, the late afternoon sunlight dancing on its surface as a breeze began to blow.

"In our tradition, we believe in cremating the body. The smoke from the fire carries the spirit of the deceased to their destination in the afterlife. One by one we will present our offerings or gifts to him. It's very important, though, that if you are presenting any kind of a weapon, that you break it with this hammer first." He gestured to the ceremonial hammer resting near the flat rock. "While the body is burning, we will celebrate with music, song, drinking, and dancing. I have some funerary mead that I have been saving for such an occasion, I just didn't expect to be using it so soon…" He drifted off in thought, his eyes shimmering with tears in the near fading light. He cleared his throat and wiped his face before continuing.

"The celebration will continue until dawn. I will then collect his ashes into an urn and carry it to the top of that hill." He pointed to a gentle slope that rose behind him. "I will bury the urn in front of a rune stone that I placed there many years ago. Anyone who wishes to accompany me to the top of the hill is welcome to do so."

The group nodded together in silent agreement to the instructions that were given to them.

"The sun is getting ready to set, so let's get this fire going."

Loki stood up with William and Rayme following him, taking their positions around the pyre and igniting the kindling stuffed between the logs of juniper, pine, and cottonwood. Rayme struggled to get his lighter to stay lit at first, and after a few failed tries, he was able to bring about a flame. The organized stack of wood crackled and popped as the flames took off and engulfed it in enormous waves, reaching high into the air, forcing them to take a step back.

Jule could feel the heat of the fire breathing on her face. It was still too early in the day and still too hot to enjoy the fire's added warmth. She gave herself some distance and sat down near the lightning-scarred tree. William plopped down in the dirt next to her and wrapped his arm gently around her neck, pulling her towards him for an awkward sideways hug. She looked up into his soft blue eyes feeling proud *this* was to be her mate, such a kind, thoughtful and strong man.

Loki removed a five-gallon glass jug filled with an amber liquid and several ale horns, placing one special, ornate gold-tipped horn in the curve of Bradley's crossed arm. The group gathered near him, taking their horns one by one and filling them to the brim with Loki's mead. They held up their horns together in a circle and cheered. Jule watched as everyone greedily gulped down their beverage. She sniffed the mysterious new alcohol, the pungent aroma stung her nose. For an alcohol made from honey, this liquid didn't smell sweet to her at all. She took a slow sip, anticipating the taste to be as bitter as the smell. Much to her surprise, and delight, the warm liquid was smooth and sweet with a tangy after-taste that left a tingling sensation in her stomach. Enjoying this new experience she, too, greedily gulped down the mead, sipping out every drop.

Rayme laid his horn down on the top of a tree stump and trotted off to his van, opening the back passenger door and pulling out several instruments. With two drums strapped over one shoulder, a guitar strapped over the other shoulder and a lute in hand, he struggled to close the door, balancing on one foot while kicking it shut with the other.

"Yes! Let's play some music while we're waiting for the fire," Loki said cheerfully while snagging the lute from Rayme's hands.

William took the guitar as Rayme offered it to him and began strumming the strings and winding the knobs to tune it. Rayme sat near Loki and passed a drum to Jeremy, keeping the remaining drum for himself. They joined together harmoniously in a song never practiced before, the sound flowing together in rhythmic melody. Fidelia stood up and began to sing a sorrowful song in Gaelic that, although was sung in a language Jule couldn't understand, resonated deep in her heart. The fire danced and flickered with the music as the sun set and darkness fell.

The pyre, now a crackling pile of hot coal, was ready to accept the body. Loki stood up and removed the heavy cloak from the gurney, revealing Bradley for the first time. The smell of decay escaped the cover and in combination with the ceremonial oils, the unpleasant odor filled Jule's nostrils. She immediately covered her nose with her hand and held her breath.

"The oils and preparations only mask the smell, I'm afraid," Loki explained.

Jule looked upon the body resting on what she now realized was a *wooden* gurney placed on a wheeled metal platform. He was dressed in a clean, dark green tunic with a white lace undershirt. A thin brown leather braided belt wrapped around his waist, the loose ends draped at his side. Knee-high black leather handcrafted boots laced up to his knees with tan cotton pants tucked neatly in. His arms crossed over his chest and his hair was braided into two locks resting on his shoulders. Like Jeff, the body was just a *shell* of what Bradley was – an empty vessel void of spirit.

"If you girls would be so kind as to gather those herbs in the bags and place them around Bradley's body..." Loki asked. "And those of you who have brought weaponry as offerings, now is the time to break them with the hammer on the rock to release your spirit from the item."

Jule, Esadora, and Fidelia grabbed two bags of herbs each and began sifting through the foliage, laying them decoratively around Bradley's resting body, crowning his head with lavender and rosemary, tucking the mint and sage beneath him. Jule combined a bundle of each herb and placed it neatly in Bradley's folded hands.

As the last stalk of rosemary was placed delicately at his side, the girls stood up in unison and Jule parted from them, unfastening her belt to remove the offering she brought, removed the blade from its protective sheath and laid it across the stone. She picked up the heavy steel hammer and smashed the dagger, chipping the blade and cracking the handle. One by one, each of them placed their gifts next to Bradley on his bed of herbs. Loki laid a Nordic steel sword in an elegant sheath that shimmered in the light of the fire across Bradley's chest. William presented an antique hunting bow carved with the depiction of a bull elk bugling and quiver to match. Esadora draped a beautiful black and white handmade silk scarf with runic lettering stitched along the edges over his hands. Fidelia rested a black wooden staff topped with the carving of a raven's head in incredible detail along his side. Jeremy set a white-handled curved ceremonial blade at his hip. Athan placed a beautiful ornate emerald scarab pendant at the base of his throat. Jule gently placed her dagger alongside the sword.

Loki, Rayme, William, Athan, and Jeremy carefully lifted the wooden gurney and placed it in the middle of the hot, burning coals. Each one then took more lumber from the stack nearby and added more fuel to the fire, bringing the flames back to life. The fire engulfed Bradley's body, smoke rising high into the air.

Loki turned and faced the small crowd.

"I will now honor the goddess Freya with a prayer," he began. Loki cleared his throat, held his arms up high towards the rising smoke.

"Hail Freya," he called out to the skies. "Goddess and Queen of the Valkyrie. A warrior awaits your guidance. Welcome him to join my ancestors so that he may rest in Honor. Oh great Queen of love, war, and beauty; Battle Maid strong and wise, I honor you now with this rite. Guide my brother home."

Loki ended his prayer with a few words in Nordic murmured under his breath, then dropped his hands to his sides.

A pile of ash lay where the pyre cremated Bradley's body throughout the night. The mead was spent and the mourners were exhausted from a night of celebration. A bright orange beam of light from the rising sun broke over the peak and dropped down onto the lake. Loki stood up and retrieved the tightly wrapped object from the base of the lightning-scarred tree and unraveled it, revealing an old ceramic urn etched with Nordic boats, axes, and runes. Using a large wooden spoon he carefully scooped up the ashes and placed them inside the urn. The group watched in silence.

With the last scoop added, Loki sealed the urn tight and returned to his feet. He took a deep sigh as he looked upon the urn cradled in his arms.

William approached him and placed a hand heavily on his shoulder.

"Are you ready?" William asked.

"Yes," Loki said quietly. "Let's put my brother in his final resting place."

Loki led the way as Jule and William followed hand-in-hand, the rest of the group staying behind to clean up. The rocky trail weaved between juniper and pine trees which seemed to part as Loki approached, making way for him to pass. The cool morning breeze tickled the back of Jule's neck, sending a chill down her spine.

At last they reached the peak topped with a large runic stone half-buried in the dirt. Jule released William's hand and approached the edge of the cliff-side. She admired the vast view, looking down over the Gila wilderness for miles and miles, a sea of green shifting to and fro as the wind blew through the canyon tossing the pinon and juniper wildly about. Two black hawks soared circling above, the white stripe at the tip of the tail shining brightly against their blackish-brown feathers.

Loki knelt at the base of the stone, placing his free hand on the top of it and closing his eyes with his head bowed, cradling the urn lovingly in the nook of his arm. With a deep breath, he scooted back and began digging a hole with his bare hands. William knelt down beside him and dug with him. When Loki was satisfied with the depth of the hole, he gently placed the urn inside and buried it, piling nearby slate rocks on top.

"Farewell, Brother," he said. "Until we meet again."

William wrapped his arm around Jule as they stood next to Loki gazing out into the wilds. The wind whipped about them wildly, tossing Jule's hair into her face. Peace washed over Loki's face as he closed his eyes, took in a deep breath, and turned his face to soak up the morning sun.

"So, what now?" Jule asked.

William smiled wide and looked down at her.

"How do you feel about meeting other lycans?" he grinned.

MORE THAN HUMAN

About the Author

Heather is a plant-enthusiast living on a quiet farm in New Mexico. She spends much of her time gardening and caring for her many animals. Heather is a loving mother of three, devoted wife, and entrepreneur who also enjoys photography.

www.facebook.com/H.AshburyAuthor
HeatherAshbury89@gmail.com

Made in the USA
Middletown, DE
28 October 2023

41553621R00106